DANCE ME A DREAM

KAIT NOLAN

Dance Me A Dream

Written and published by Kait Nolan

Cover design by Lori Jackson

Copyright 2016 Kait Nolan

Once Upon a Snow Day

Written and published by Kait Nolan

Copyright 2013 Kait Nolan

A LETTER TO READERS

Dear Reader,

This book is set in the Deep South. As such, it contains a great deal of colorful, colloquial, and occasionally grammatically incorrect language. This is a deliberate choice on my part as an author to most accurately represent the region where I have lived my entire life. While this particular book contains little swearing and no pre-marital sex between the lead couple, most of my work does, as those things are part of the realistic lives of characters of this generation, and of many of my readers.

If any of these things are not your cup of tea, please consider that you may not be the right audience for this book. There are scores of other books out there that are written with you in mind. In fact, I've got a list of some of my favorite authors who write on the sweeter side on my website at https://kaitnolan.com/on-the-sweeter-side/

If you choose to stick with me, I hope you enjoy!

Happy reading!

Kait

CHAPTER 1

FROST GLISTENED ON THE carved stone of the fountain that was the jewel of the Wishful town green, looking candied and fanciful, like something out of a fairy tale. Tara Honeycutt hunched her shoulders against the cold, watching her breath puff out in clouds. She really needed to get going. The window between when she dropped her siblings off at school and when she had to be at The Daily Grind for her shift was already narrow, and today she needed to swing by to pick up a check for her sales at the artisan market where she sold her hand-crafted jewelry. But the fountain had drawn her. Maybe because of the dream.

Last night she'd been back in her old life. On the stage. Preparing for the season's opening performance of *The Nutcracker*. She'd woken out of sorts, with a gut-deep yearning for what used to be. And so, here she was, a coin in her fist, about to make a wish in the fountain that gave the town its name.

I wish...

What did she wish? Did she really want to go back to professional dance? To the brutal schedule? The grueling competition? The loneliness? No. Whatever she may have missed about performing, it wasn't that. She'd traded her career for family and she wouldn't—couldn't—go back on that.

But God, to be a normal twenty-one year old girl, free of all these responsibilities...

I wish I could be normal girl, just for a little while.

Tara tossed the coin into the water and immediately felt guilty for making such a selfish wish. She found herself digging into her purse for another coin.

I'll just make another wish. Surely that's not breaking the rules.

Clutching this one tight in her hand, Tara stared hard at the fountain, as if that would somehow impress upon whatever powers that be that she was really serious about this one.

I wish I could give Austin and Ginny a good Christmas. The kind of Christmas they truly deserve.

The nickel hit the water with a thunk, joining the legion of others from wishers who'd come before.

Okay, that was enough of that foolishness. She needed to get going. With long-legged strides, she headed across the green toward Wishful Discount Drugs.

The historic downtown pharmacy was decked out for the holidays in true Currier and Ives style, with swags of greenery, twinkly lights, and festoons of ribbon. The windows had been flocked with fake snow, and somebody had even found a vintage Christmas village to set up in the front window. Tara made a mental note to bring the kids by to see it. Ginny would absolutely love it, and even Austin would be charmed by the train circling on a track. Bing Crosby crooned "White Christmas" over the loudspeakers as Tara stepped inside.

"Be with you in a sec!" Pharmacist Riley Gower's voice floated from somewhere below counter level.

Tara crossed over, trying to think if she needed to pick up anything else while she was here. Ginny's insulin supply was good, and they'd just restocked syringes last week.

Riley popped up, a pair of felt reindeer antlers perched in her glossy dark brown hair. "Tara! Merry Christmas!"

Tara grinned. "Nice antlers."

"I drew the line at the nose."

"I think the rosy cheeks and sparkle in your eyes make up for it. They've been a permanent addition since you and Liam got engaged."

Riley beamed and blushed. "I keep thinking I'll get used to it. But I don't."

"Don't ever get used to it. I think that's the key to staying in love. And it looks good on you," Tara added. If she felt just a wee pinch of envy, it wasn't big enough to note. Riley and Liam were two of her favorite people—kind and generous to a fault. Tara was delighted they'd found each other.

But a tiny part of her—the small, self-absorbed part wishing for a normal life—wondered if she'd ever get the chance to find someone of her own. At least before her siblings were grown and out on their own. What did the dating scene look like for thirty-two year olds? It didn't bear thinking about.

"I'll get your check. You've had absolutely outstanding sales. If you've got any other stock to load in, now's the time. The last minute shoppers are picking up and everybody's loving the new artisan market."

"I've got a few more things I can bring by in a day or two."

Riley disappeared into the office.

If she stayed up a couple extra hours tonight, she could probably stretch that to more. Tara's mind was already spinning new jewelry designs based on the supplies she had left when Riley came back out.

"Here we go." She handed over the check.

Tara took it. "Thanks. I've gotta jet. I'm gonna be late to my shift at The Grind and we've been hopping with all the holiday shoppers."

"I'll see you in a few days when you bring in the new stock."

Tara turned toward the door, glancing down at the check. She took in the number of zeroes. Blinked. Looked again. "You forgot to take out the booth rental fee."

"Nope. The amount is right. You've sold out all but two pieces."

Tara stared at her. "You're kidding."

"Make that all but one," Jessie Applewhite said. Riley's pharmacy tech wandered in from the market side of the store. "I'm nabbing that turquoise pendant necklace right now. And if Eli comes in looking for ideas, I want the earrings, too. Just sayin'."

"Well, sweet little baby Jesus," Tara muttered.

"Told you. Enjoy it!" Riley urged.

Two wishes, one of them answered in fifteen minutes. That had to be some kind of record. Batting 500—and the more important 500 at that—was pretty darn good odds. She didn't have a prayer of a shot at being a normal girl, but this year—this year she'd be able to give her brother and sister a *real* Christmas. One with new traditions and festivities that would make up, at least a little, for the absence of their parents.

Tucking the check carefully into her purse, Tara hurried to work.

THERE'S *no place like home.*

Jace Applewhite took his time crossing the

town green, enjoying the sight of the enormous town Christmas tree. The Bradford pears lining Main Street were wrapped in twinkle lights, and the light poles had regimented lines of lit wreaths marching all the way around the green. Beautiful. And with the unseasonably cold weather, it actually felt like winter. Of course, give it a day or two and it'd be 75 degrees. Such was the nature of December in Mississippi. His sister Livia and their cousin Jessie had a long-running bet on whether they'd be able to wear t-shirts for Christmas Day.

Jace stepped into The Daily Grind, scanning the faces for his friends. Grad school exams had wrapped a bit earlier than expected, so he'd come on home to Wishful to help with the family business for the remainder of the holiday. He'd head out to the farm and surprise his parents after catching up with the guys.

Across the room, Eli lifted his hand in a wave.

"Well, you're a sight for sore eyes," Jace said, pulling him into a back thumping hug.

"That's what you get for doing the grad school thing, man. Lots of tiny print. While you're up to your eyeballs in textbooks, I'm out in the good clean air."

"And how's the Forestry Service treating you?"

"Can't complain," Eli said.

"How's my cousin treating you? Or maybe I should ask how you're treating Jessie."

"He's whipped," Zach Warren announced, rising from his chair to repeat the man hug routine.

"As he should be. She's too good for him. Where are Leo and Reed?"

"Leo's running the lighting and sound for the community theater's production of *White Christmas*, and Reed is in Connecticut with his lady love and her parents."

"I still can't believe he's engaged," Jace murmured.

"Brother, you and me both," Eli said.

"You worried Jessie's gonna get ideas?"

Eli's face paled. "Dude, don't even talk about that. We haven't been dating *that* long."

Laughing, Jace slapped him on the shoulder. "Only a matter of time, buddy. Let me grab some coffee." Jace joined the short queue at the counter, tapping a finger against his leg in time with the rhythm of the music playing over the sound system. What was that? *Charlie Brown Christmas?*

"Welcome to The Daily Grind. What can I get you?"

Jace focused on the girl behind the counter. *Your number.*

Tall and willowy, her sandy blonde hair was piled on top of her head in some updo that left her long, graceful neck bare. His fingers itched to trace it, to see if her skin was as soft as it looked. Her hazel eyes were expectant, and Jace realized he hadn't said anything. He cleared his throat. "Um, what do you recommend?"

"For light roast today, we've got a Nku-rubuye from Rawanda. Our dark roast is an

Idido from Ethiopia. This late in the day, I'd be inclined to go for the dark. Less caffeine."

"Really? I thought darker roasts had more caffeine."

"Other way around," she said. The name tag on her holly red apron read *Tara*. "The roasting process destroys some of the caffeine, so the lighter the roast, the more potent."

Her voice was deeper than he expected. A throaty, rich alto. Talk about potent.

"I'll have the dark then. Just black."

Tara punched at the iPad mounted at the register. "Any nibbles to go with it?"

Jace could think of several of her inches he'd like to nibble. Jesus, he really had been stuck in a book too damned long. "No, nothing to eat, thanks."

Her slender fingers punched in the rest of the transaction and tipped the iPad toward him to pay. "I'll just get this started for you."

Jace pulled out his wallet and swiped his card before he forgot how to use it. Tara seemed to float across the floor, graceful and unhurried, almost like a dance. How did she do that?

"Here you go."

He took the steaming mug she offered. "You aren't from around here."

She tipped her head in question.

"I'd remember if I'd seen you before," Jace clarified.

"You haven't been in for coffee in a year and a half? I know all the regulars."

"Grad school at Mississippi State," he explained. "I've been having my caffeine directly by IV drip."

Her lips curved a little, and Jace found himself wanting to see her full smile. He'd bet it was stunning.

"Home for the holidays, then," she concluded, friendly but not exactly a green light to his flirtation.

"I am indeed. A full month until I have to go back. I'll be one of those regulars before you know it." Jace grinned, hoping she'd respond in kind.

But Tara wasn't quite paying attention. Her head angled slightly, her eyes unfocused and heartbreakingly sad.

The sight of it struck a deep, painful chord in him, reminding him of another pair of somber eyes. He wanted to reach out and stroke her cheek. *Don't be sad.* The music on the sound system had shifted to *The Nutcracker*. Not exactly a melancholy tune.

Before he could work that out, she shook herself, plastering on a smile that was stiff around the edges. "You have a merry Christmas."

It was a polite brush off with an underlying message of *hands off.*

"You, too," Jace murmured, lifting the coffee in a toast and heading back to his friends.

"Need a fire extinguisher?" Eli asked.

"Huh?"

"Because you just crashed and burned, brother."

Jace glanced back at Tara, who was helping another customer. "What's her story? Is she seeing somebody?" Which was only half what he wanted to know. He wanted—needed—to know what had put that look in her eyes.

"Oh no, the Snow Queen shoots down all comers," Eli said. "Many have tried. No one has succeeded."

"Snow Queen? Isn't that kinda harsh?" Jace felt offended on Tara's behalf.

"She's never rude, just kind of holds herself apart. More important things to worry about than dating."

"You're taken," Jace reminded him. "By my cousin."

"I'm off the market. I'm not blind," Eli protested.

Zach picked up the thread. "She's been here a bit over a year, I think. Not sure where she came from, but she's got guardianship of her two half-siblings."

"She's young for that isn't she?" Jace didn't think she was more than twenty-two.

"Got them at nineteen."

"Holy crap. Why?"

Zach sipped at his coffee. "Mom left for parts unknown a few years back. And their dad is in jail on burglary charges. Tara's the only other family they've got."

That was certainly adequate reason to be sad. "Wow. How old are the kids?"

"Third grade and fifth from what I remember when I did school pics earlier this fall," Zach reported.

So, for the time being, anyway, she was a single sort-of mom. The hands off vibe made total sense in that context. Jace should probably respect that. But as he sat catching up with his friends, he knew he'd spend the next month feeding his coffee habit.

CHAPTER 2

*T*ARA'S EYE CRACKED OPEN and searched out the time on the LED clock by her bedside. 9:30.

Ohmygod. She rocketed out of bed and tripped down the hall, cursing the action figures and Legos in the floor. They were going to be so late to school!

Ginny looked up with wide blue eyes from her bean bag by the coffee table, her blocky stuffed bear, Lump tucked under her arm. Bugs Bunny sassed Elmer Fudd on the screen. Austin sketched at the kitchen table. He didn't even glance her way as she came skidding into the room.

"Why didn't you wake me?"

"'Cause it's Saturday?" Ginny suggested .

"Oh." Tara scooped a hand through her hair. The last week had flown by, full of late nights knocking out several new pieces to take to the artisan market. Her body clock was all screwed up and she'd lost track of days. In the wake of the adrenaline burst that had propelled her out of bed, she felt the exhaustion that had been dogging her for days.

Neither of the kids was in need of medical attention and nothing was broken or otherwise destroyed, so they'd managed to quietly entertain themselves, while she slept in for the first time in...who knew how long.

"Y'all had breakfast?"

"Cereal," Austin said.

Tara looked sharply in his direction.

"No sugar on Ginny's," he added, though he still didn't look up from his drawing.

Okay then. She'd slept in for three hours

and the world had not stopped. Surely that miracle would last long enough for her to caffeinate.

Bugs Bunny gave way to Wile E. Coyote by the time she came back into the living room with a cup of tea. The ancient sofa sank beneath her weight. Mug in hand, Tara looked around the living room. Toys littered the old shag carpet, but she'd managed a fresh coat of paint on the walls back in the summer. Austin's artwork hung in an informal gallery on one of them, something he'd acted annoyed by but she knew he secretly loved. All the furniture was worn. She'd refinished the wood pieces in a distressed cottage style that suited life with kids. The bright pillows accenting the sofa and chairs perked up the space. It helped, but there was no masking the fact that the house was old and hadn't been cared for as it should've in the years before she moved in.

Maybe after she finished shopping for the kids, she'd swing by the local thrift store and see if they had a decent couch that fit into her budget.

Ginny crawled up beside her and curled into Tara's side, snuggling in like an overlarge cat. Tara stroked her sister's silky hair and felt her heart roll over in her chest. She'd come a long, long way from the terrified and distrustful little girl who'd suddenly found herself living with an older sister she'd only met a couple of times. Austin was slower to warm up and he still spent more of his time lost in his own head, sullen and angry over their circumstances. But he argued less and was more inclined to help with Ginny than resent her, so that, too, was progress.

"So I thought we'd decorate for Christmas this weekend. What do y'all think about that?"

Austin jerked a shoulder. "Whatever."

Ginny sat up. "Can we make popcorn garland?"

Tara pegged her with an amused look. "Do you actually want popcorn garland or do you just want popcorn?"

"Both."

"Then I suppose we can do popcorn garland. What about you, Austin?"

"No amount of popcorn is going to cover up that ugly fake tree."

Her little brother had a deep and abiding hatred of the fake Christmas tree they'd had the year before. Tara had found it in the attic and done what she could to nurse the Charlie Brown tree into something festive, but even her artistic skills had been challenged by that.

"You're absolutely right. Which is why we are aren't going to use the ugly fake tree."

"So we're not having a tree?" Ginny's lip wobbled.

"We're not having a *fake* tree," Tara corrected. "This year we're going to get a real one."

Austin finally looked up at that, a fleeting expression of hope on his face before he shut down again. "We can't afford a real tree. They're a waste of money."

Hearing what she knew were their father's words falling out of his mouth, Tara felt a fresh wave of rage whip through her. He hadn't done right by these kids. Not ever. When she was sure she could speak without swearing, she said, "Well, whether they're a waste or not is a matter of opinion. But as it happens we're doing okay this Christmas, and we're going to have a real tree."

"Won't all the lots be picked over? It's only two weeks to Christmas."

"Probably. That's why we're going out to Applewhite Farms to cut a fresh one ourselves." It was so much more expensive, but by damn, she was going to give them some good Christmas memories.

"Really?" Ginny's eyes got even rounder. "I've heard stories about that place. Becca says they have hot chocolate and horses and lights and everything!"

"Well, I don't know if they'll have lights and stuff during the day, but I'm sure they'll have something. And it'll be fun to walk the fields and pick our very own tree. What do you say?"

"Yay!"

She patted Ginny on the rump. "Go get dressed. Both of you. If we get the tree this morning, we can spend the afternoon making more ornaments."

Her sister bolted down the hall to her bedroom.

Tara looked back at her brother. "Austin? You up for the whole cutting a live tree experience?"

"That could be cool."

An almost positive statement. Tara would take it.

JACE LOVED quiet mornings on the farm. Other times of year, when it was the apple or pecan groves that were their bread and butter, mornings meant work. But when it came time for Christmas, the Fraser Firs and Scotch Pines were far less demanding. After four, they'd have steady traffic the rest of the night as the last minute folks came in search of a tree. But for now, it was just him and the trees. Livia had already gone in to work at the library where she ran the children's program. Dad had headed to the Co-op to pick up a part for the tractor, and Mom was puttering around in the kitchen, baking up cookies for the legion of people she gifted them to for the holidays.

He was working on his second cup of coffee when the little SUV came up the drive. They weren't officially open until this afternoon, but not everybody knew that. The driver slowed near the house, then pulled to a stop over near the main barn. The driver's side door opened and one long leg stretched out, followed by the rest of a tall blonde. She opened the rear passenger door and a little girl tumbled out, vibrating with excitement. The blonde took her hand as an older boy climbed out of the front seat. It was just one little family. He could deal with that. Jace stepped down from the porch and headed over.

"Mornin'," he called.

The blonde turned and he was delighted to

meet the gorgeous hazel eyes of his coffeeshop crush. "Jace."

"Hey Tara." In the week he'd been home, he'd gone in to The Grind for coffee almost every day. Enough that she recognized him now, even if he hadn't gotten any further than giving her his name.

"I didn't know you worked out here."

Translation: *I didn't come looking for you, so don't start up with that flirting again.*

He repressed a smile. "Comes with the last name."

"Which is?"

"Applewhite. This is my family's farm."

"You're related to Livia. Or Jessie?"

Small town. Of course she knew them. "Both. Liv's my sister. Jessie's my cousin."

"Oh." She seemed to cast around for something else to say. "We came for a tree."

Jace looked up at the clear blue sky. "It's a fine morning for it. And you'll have the place to yourselves since it's not Saturday."

Tara startled. "It's not?"

"Nope. Friday."

She shot a Look at the little girl. "Ginny."

The little girl grinned like an imp. "What?"

"You said it was Saturday! And you didn't contradict her," she said to the boy.

He shrugged. "It's nothin' but stupid parties at school today. We're not missing anything important."

Something flickered over Tara's face. Distress? Some kind of understanding? Jace wondered what was going through her head.

"Well then, I guess we're playing hookey today." She turned back to him. "But you're not open until four. I'm sorry. I've been running around all morning thinking it's Saturday."

"It's not a problem," Jace assured her. "You're already here. Might as well pick a tree."

Ginny bounced. "It's our first real tree ever! We have to pick the best one!"

"First one, huh?" He looked to Tara. "You in a hurry?"

"No, I don't suppose so. I need to call in to work, though."

"In that case, y'all should have the first timer's special. Come on into the barn out of the cold and make your call, while I get things set up." Without waiting for agreement, he went on inside.

Ginny's eyes got huge when he led Pepper out of the stall. "Ohmygod. It's a horse!"

"This is Pepper. She helps pull the wagon for our hayrides." The chestnut mare bumped her nose at his jacket where she knew he had some carrots. Jace scratched between her ears. "Want to feed her?"

"Can I really?" Ginny whispered.

"If it's okay with your sister."

Tara, who'd just finished her call, looked sharply in his direction.

Jace pretended not to notice.

"Be careful," she said.

He showed Ginny how to hold her hand flat and placed a piece of carrot on her little palm. She giggled as Pepper carefully picked it up. "Her whiskers tickle. Austin, you gotta try this!"

"You can treat Rupert. We have to be fair or I'll hear about it."

Rupert stuck his head over the stall and nickered.

"See?"

Jace led the gelding out as well and tied him to a ring mounted on the wall. He repeated the demonstration for how Austin should hold his hand and handed over a piece of carrot. Some of the apathy slipped from the boy's expression as Rupert mouthed up his treat. He ran a hand down the horse's glossy brown coat.

"Austin, you want to help me carry the harnesses?"

"Sure."

As he went through the process of getting both horses hitched to the wagon, Jace was aware of Tara watching him. But he kept his attention on the kids, the animals. She didn't want flirtation; he'd try another tactic. Besides, he got a kick out of Ginny's enthusiasm. He lifted her in to the wagon bed. "Up we go."

Austin climbed in himself.

Jace turned to Tara. "You want to ride in the back or up front with me?"

"I don't much fancy hay poking me in the behind, so I'll take the seat."

He leapt up and held out a hand for her. After a moment's hesitation, she took it, seeming to flow almost like water as he pulled her. For a couple of long seconds they stood a handspan apart. She was tall, only a few inches shorter than him, and he was very aware that it'd take almost no effort to close the distance between them. He was also aware of her two younger siblings less than five feet away, so though he wanted to linger, Jace released her as soon as she was steady.

His mother came out on the porch as he gathered up the reins and clucked at the horses to head out. She lifted one hand in a wave. There would be questions later, but he'd endure them. It was worth it for the excited stream of questions and chatter from Ginny and the un-guarded look of pleasure Tara beamed over her shoulder at the kids.

"Dashing through the snow."

Beside him, Tara startled when he began to sing.

"On a one horse open sleigh. Ginny?"

"Over the fields we go, laughing all the way! Ha ha ha!" she shouted, joining in with more enthusiasm than correct pitch.

"Bells on bobtail ring."

Tara jumped in. "Making spirits bright."

"What fun it is to laugh and sing a sleighing song tonight."

They picked up Austin on the chorus and the four of them belted good cheer into the late morning air, startling some birds from the trees in the apple orchard as they rolled through. A rendition of "Rudolph The Red-Nosed Reindeer" got them to the edge of the fir trees.

Jace drove the horses down the center lane before pulling them to a halt. "Now we walk."

Tara leapt down before he could help her, but Ginny waited, arms outstretched for him to lift her down.

"How tall are your ceilings?" Jace asked.

"Just the standard eight feet."

He pulled one of their premarked measuring sticks and handed it over to Austin.

"What's this for?"

"See this mark? That's seven feet. In a stand, that's about as tall as you can go with your ceilings. You hold this next to the trees to check and see if they'll fit."

"Okay. C'mon, Ginny!"

The pair of them scampered down the row, Ginny launching into an off-key rendition of "Frosty The Snowman".

"She hasn't quite mastered the difference between singing and shouting," Tara said. "They're loving this. Thank you."

Jace retrieved the axe and headed after them, Tara falling into step beside him. "You're more than welcome. There's hot apple cider when we get back. Made from our own apples."

"Oh, you don't have to go to any trouble."

"No trouble. Just part of the package. You brought them out here for the whole live tree experience, right?"

Again, something flickered over her face. "Yes. They'll be talking about this for weeks."

"We like making it into people's memory books and family traditions."

"We're working on starting some new ones." Tara's expression was fierce as she said it.

Jace recognized a vow when he heard it. "Gotta be hard on you. All that responsibility."

He got that sharp look again.

"You're too young to be Mom. You and Ginny have the same eyes. I figured sister." He'd known already but didn't see the sense in confirming her expectation that people were talking.

Ahead of them Austin and Ginny raced from one tree to the next. Tara watched them for a moment before answering. "Half-sister, actually. We share a father, such as he is. As it happens, I lucked out more in the mom department than they did. So I'm working on making up for that."

"I'd say you're doing an admirable job."

Tara frowned at him. "You aren't at all put off by them, are you?"

"Not a bit. I love kids. They're a lot of fun. Especially this time of year."

"Tara come look! This one! This one!" Ginny waved her arms like she was presenting a prize.

Her sister walked around the tree, checking the shape. "How's the height?"

Austin held up the measuring stick. "Little over seven feet, but it'll fit."

"Well, I guess this is it then," Tara confirmed.

"My axe is at your service, milady. Stand back, y'all." He made short work of chopping down the tree. "We'll clean up the base once we get it back to the barn."

They retrieved the wagon and loaded up the tree. Jace took the long way back, giving an informal tour of the farm on the way.

As predicted, his mom had hot cider waiting. Jace made introductions.

"Mom, this is Tara, Austin, and Ginny Honeycutt. Y'all, my mom, Linda Applewhite."

"Nice to meet y'all." She passed out drinks, while he hauled the tree over to the baling table and smoothed out the base with the chainsaw.

"You want the trimmings?" he asked Tara.

"Yes, please."

He trimmed the lower branches enough for a stand, then pulled the whole thing through the big round tube of the baler, wrapping it in netting that would keep it bundled until they got it home. Hefting the tree on one shoulder, he hauled it over to the little SUV and tied it to the roof rack with twine.

"You're all set."

"How much do we owe you?" Tara asked.

He named a figure and accepted the cash she handed over. "I hope you enjoy it. Are you okay to get it down and in when you get home?"

"I'll manage. Thanks for everything, Jace. And thank you for the cider, Mrs. Applewhite."

"Thank you!" the kids chorused.

"Come on, you monkeys. Load up. We've got a tree to decorate."

They piled into the car. Tara shot him a

wave before she backed up and headed down the drive.

"You didn't charge them for the hay ride," Linda observed.

"Take it out of my paycheck."

CHAPTER 3

AUSTIN DRAPED COLORED TWINKLE lights around the tree. "That was so awesome! Did you see the way Jace used that axe? Chopped this thing down in three strikes. Someday I'm gonna be big enough to do that."

Yes. Yes I noticed. Tara told herself her mouth was watering over the popcorn she was stringing onto fishing line. She hadn't been able to avoid noticing the flex and bunch of muscle as he'd wielded the axe to fell their tree. She'd never known she had a secret lumberjack fantasy until this morning. A lumberjack with big brown eyes and a mile wide soft spot for kids.

It wasn't what she'd expected from a twenty-four year old grad student. She'd done her homework, too. Not that it'd been hard. Her boss, Cassie Callister, was the self-declared Princess of Gossip in Wishful, second only to Mama Pearl Buckley, who owned Dinner Belles Diner. The two were in a constant competition to find out the scoop on anything and every-thing before anybody else. In this case, Cassie had given a hopeful eyebrow waggle that the inside scoop was about Tara being interested in Jace. She'd shut down that assumption in a hurry. Even if Wishful was the family seat, he didn't live here. Not permanently. And aside from that, she didn't have time for dating or re-lationships. Besides, what guy in her age bracket would want a package deal?

The kind of guy who would go out of his way to take you all out to pick a Christmas tree, even though the farm was closed.

She'd wondered initially if Jace was just

being nice to her siblings to try to get to her since his more direct flirtation hadn't worked. But he'd seemed to genuinely enjoy hanging out with them. Austin and Ginny hadn't stopped talking about him or the farm since they got back in the car.

"Do you think we could maybe go back sometime and take Pepper and Rupert more carrots?" Ginny asked. "Horses ought to get Christmas presents, don't you think?"

"Oh, well, we'll have to see about that." Tara took great care not to make promises she wasn't positive she could keep. They'd had far too many broken in the past.

Jace may have been kind enough to give them all a great Christmas memory, but that certainly didn't mean he was ready to entertain them again.

Still, Tara couldn't regret the expressions of sheer delight on Ginny and Austin's faces. This was the most excitement she'd seen from her brother in the year and a half they'd been under her care. It was the first time he'd really acted like the kid he was. Tara figured she owed Jace something for that. If she baked him cookies would he read too much into it?

"Are you done with the popcorn garland?" Austin asked.

"Not by half. Ginny keeps eating the components."

Her sister giggled and stuffed another handful of popcorn into her mouth.

Shaking her head with a smile, Tara headed for the kitchen. "I'll go make another batch."

An enormous boom shook the house. Tara automatically dove to cover Ginny, yelling for Austin to get down.

But no glass rained down. There were no aftershocks. No scent of smoke.

Austin peeked out from behind the Christmas tree. "What was that?"

"I don't know. Maybe a transformer blew." *It totally wasn't a transformer.* That explosion had been way too loud. "Everybody okay?"

"Yeah, fine."

"I'm okay." Ginny squirmed out of Tara's

hold and made a beeline for the window. "There's smoke over there."

Tara followed where she pointed, seeing billowing smoke in the distance above the treeline. "Y'all, put on your shoes and coats. We're gonna go find out what's going on."

While the kids gathered their stuff, she stepped out onto the porch. Whatever was burning was far enough off she didn't feel like the house was in immediate danger. They'd had a wet autumn, so the woods between here and there shouldn't go up like tinder. But something big had blown.

Bundling the kids into the RAV, she locked the house and headed up the road. As soon as the trees cleared, she could see the huge towers of flame fanning the sky.

"Holy crap!"

Tara was too shocked to correct her brother. Holy crap, indeed.

Even as she stared, a fire truck approached from the rear. She pulled over to the shoulder behind another vehicle to let it pass, then just sat there. The driver of the car in front got out and walked up to the window.

Tara rolled it down and heard the roar. "Any idea what's going on?"

"Gas line exploded," he said, turning to look back toward where the firemen were unfurling hose and spraying down the blaze. "I heard it over the scanner. They're calling in fire crews from all over the county."

"Gas? Oh man, our house runs on gas. Is it safe?"

"Tara! Lump!" Ginny wailed from the back seat.

"Hush, honey. Lump will be okay."

"The damage to the line is two miles from here. If they haven't already, the gas company will be shutting down the supply to help contain the fire. Thankfully there aren't any houses right around the fire."

"Thank God for small mercies." They weren't equipped to recover from a fire.

"The bigger question is how long it'll take them to repair it. I don't think that's one of the main lines, but that was a pretty big mess. It'll take some doing to get it back up and running."

That introduced a whole new set of worries. They had gas heat, gas water heater, and gas stove. She could manage the cooking via microwave and toaster oven. And she'd bundle the kids into the living room for a family snuggle fest with the couple of space heaters they had. But they'd only be able to rough it for a couple of days. If the repairs took longer than that, they'd be screwed.

"Hey little brother."

One hand on the door to The Daily Grind, Jace cursed Livia's proclivity toward being early for everything. But he fixed a smile on his face as he turned to greet her. "Hey big sis." He wrapped an arm around her in a hug.

"So, Mom tells me there's a girl."

"There's no girl." There wasn't. He hadn't

even asked Tara out, so there couldn't be a girl. Right? "How's the library treating you?"

"Could be better. Our hours are going to be cut again. I just know it."

Jace winced. The Wishful Public Library had been suffering from epic budget constraints the past year and a half, a reflection of Wishful's languishing economy. Livia, the children's librarian, had been operating at three-quarter's salary for months. Given the salary was a pittance in the first place, that was very bad indeed.

"I thought things were getting better around here since the new city planner started."

"They have. But the kind of trickle down we need takes a long time. Mitzi has been doing the budgets this week and looking grim. I think I'm going to have to give up my apartment and move back home until this gets straightened out."

Pulling open the door, Jace made an after you motion. "You know Mom would be delighted to have you back for more than just tree season. She loves nothing more than having all her chicks under one roof."

"I know. And I love it out at the farm. It's just demoralizing. You aren't supposed to have to move home at twenty-seven."

"Well then, let me buy you a hot chocolate or something."

"I won't say no."

Tara stood behind the counter, chatting with a customer and Jace had to work to keep the smile off his face. He spotted the kids hanging out in a nearby booth. They hadn't seen him yet or he was sure they'd be running over to greet him.

"—doing since the gas main exploded? That's out near you, isn't it?" the customer asked.

Jace's ears perked. Like everybody else in town, he'd heard about the gas main explosion. It'd taken every fire fighter in the county to get the blaze under control.

"We're mostly fine. It wasn't close enough to do any damage to the house. But a lot of our stuff runs on gas. The heat, the stove, the water heater. The gas company said the damage was so bad, we're not going to have service again until after Christmas."

"That's awful!" said the woman.

Jace stepped around her. "What have you been doing without heat, hot water, or a way to cook?"

"Hey Jace. We've been roughing it the last few days. Camping in the living room with space heaters. That hasn't been so bad since it warmed up. We've been cleaning up in the locker rooms at the gym. And thank God for crock pots. We've been eating tons of soup. The kids look at the whole thing as an adventure, but the shine's going to wear off of that soon."

"Serious cold front's coming, too. Have you seen the forecast? They're saying we may have our first white Christmas in generations."

Tara grimaced. "Yeah, I heard. The kids are so psyched about that. But it's definitely not ideal under the circumstances. I have no idea what we're going to do if the gas company doesn't pull off some kind of Christmas miracle."

"You should come out to the farm." The words were out of his mouth before he even knew they were there.

"Excuse me?"

"We've got an apartment upstairs in one of the barns. It's usually used by seasonal staff, but this year all our help is local, so there's nobody in it now." In his periphery, Jace could see Livia giving him the side eye. "It's just a little two bedroom with a kitchenette, but it's furnished, and, more importantly, it has full utilities and heat."

He could tell before she even opened her mouth that she was going to say no. "That's very kind of you, Jace but—"

"Jace!" Ginny, finally catching sight of him, raced over from the booth, throwing her arms around his legs.

He ruffled her hair. "Hey, Peanut. What're you doing out of school?"

"It's a teacher day," she informed him. "How are Pepper and Rupert?"

"They're good. They say hi."

"I wanna say hi back," she insisted. "I asked Tara if we could bring them carrots for Christmas but she said we had to ask you first."

"You can absolutely bring Pepper and Rupert carrots for Christmas." And then Jace decided to play dirty. "I was just trying to talk your sister into bringing all of you out to the farm for Christmas as our *guests*, since y'all are out of heat." He placed extra emphasis, figuring part of her objection would be money.

Ginny's eyes got huge. "Tara! Oh can we can we can we? Ohpleaseohpleaseohplease!"

"Yeah, Tara," Austin added, "we could help with stuff at the farm."

"Sure," Jace said, getting into the idea. "I could teach you how to drive the wagon."

"For real?"

"Sure."

"That'd be awesome!"

"It's settled, then. These two will work for

their keep. We need a couple of elves around the place." Jace made a show of checking Ginny's ears for points.

Tara's expression only got stiffer. "I really appreciate it, but—"

Ginny's face crumpled and Jace could tell she was about to cry. He scooped her up and pressed his cheek to hers. "C'mon. How can you say no to this face?"

Tara's eyes narrowed. "You don't play fair," she murmured.

"He doesn't," Livia agreed. "I'm sorry to say, he learned that from me. But seriously, we'd love to have you. Having some kids around will get Mom off our backs for not having given her grandchildren yet."

"Well, I..." She trailed off, looking from Ginny to Austin before closing her eyes. Jace knew she was going to cave. "Thank you. We appreciate it."

"Hooray!"

Jace put Ginny down and the kids launched into some kind of complicated victory dance.

Tara just shook her head, a reluctant smile twitching at the corners of her mouth. "Did you actually want coffee, or were you only here to railroad me?"

"Oh coffee, absolutely," Jace said.

He and Livia gave their orders and headed for a table. "Thanks for backing me up."

"No girl, my ass," she said. "How long will it take you to move your stuff out of the apartment?"

Jace maintained an innocent expression. "Not long. And I'm just spreading the Christmas spirit."

"You're spreading something." Livia laid a hand over his. "It's a nice thing you're doing. But be careful. Those kids have been through a lot."

So had Tara. And Jace was willing to bet nobody had been thinking about helping her.

CHAPTER 4

*T*HE OLD VICTORIAN FARMHOUSE glinted like a jewel in the night as Tara pulled up. Lights and garland twined the rails, followed the eaves. The whole place looked like a postcard.

What must it be like to live out here in all of this?

And they'd be spending Christmas *here?* Tara didn't know whether to jump for joy or run away. The generosity of Jace and his family would certainly keep them warm this holiday and give all three of them cherished memories.

But what happened next year when things were back to whatever version of normal she managed for Austin and Ginny? Nothing she could do could possibly live up to all of this.

A figure came down the porch steps. Livia. A blend of relief and disappointment trickled through Tara as she got out of the RAV. She wasn't quite ready to face Jace again. She felt far too off balance around him, and that wasn't a comfortable state for Tara. "I wasn't sure where to park."

"Where you are is fine. The apartment's down here." Livia led her down a path to a smaller barn out past the one that housed Pepper and Rupert.

"Y'all really know how to do Christmas, don't you?"

Livia grinned. "It's kind of the Applewhite thing. Goes with the territory when you have a tree farm."

"I suppose it does. Do you ever get tired of it? All the hustle and bustle and forced holiday cheer?" Tara was pretty sure she was caroling in her sleep these days.

"Only when it starts the day after Halloween. The actual traditions attached to this place...nah. It's all part of marking the seasons here. And it's a privilege to be a part of so many families' holiday traditions."

"I'm sure after spending the holiday out here, the kids will be campaigning to make this a part of ours. Jace may have created a monster."

"He's a big boy. He can take care of himself. The apartment's just up those stairs. It's unlocked. Sorry to leave you here, but I've got bread coming out of the oven in a few minutes."

"No problem. Thanks again."

Livia disappeared before she could ask where her brother and sister were. With Jace, probably, given how they'd both glommed onto him like he was the best thing since peanut butter met chocolate. She'd just check the place out and breathe a minute before going to find him. *Them,* she corrected. She needed to steer clear of Jace.

Stairs went straight up to her left, just inside the barn door, then angled back right toward a railed space that began what had once probably been a hay loft. Tara sniffed, but the place didn't smell of hay, more like pine or cedar, with a faint undertone of...apples? She made her way up the stairs, glancing down at the equipment neatly stowed below. It seemed like a sort of carriage house with tractor attachments lined up in rows down the side walls.

As Livia promised, the apartment door was unlocked. She opened it, expecting to have to fumble for a light switch, and stopped dead in the doorway.

He'd brought their tree.

The fully decorated Fraser fir that'd been in her living room a few hours before now stood in a place of honor near the window, twinkle lights blinking on and off in the darkness.

Tara stared for a long moment before absently reaching to turn on a lamp. Slowly, she circled the tree, marveling that the ornaments were not only intact, they seemed to be more or less exactly where they'd been originally. How the hell had he pulled this off? And when? He'd shown up at the house just before Tara had left to go teach her 5:30 yoga class and somehow she'd been agreeing to let him take the kids and their stuff out to the farm so they wouldn't have to hang out in the gym office while she taught.

She wasn't purely sure how that happened either.

What was she even *doing* here?

Footsteps tromped up the stairs and the man himself ducked into the entryway. "Oh good, you made it. Are you finding everything okay?"

"I just got here. Livia pointed me up."

"How'd your class go?"

"Fine." Though every bit of Zen she'd earned from the practice had evaporated when he'd walked into the room.

Jace crossed to one of the doors at the back

of the apartment. "We put your stuff in here. Kids are across the hall."

Because she didn't know what else to do, Tara walked over and peered into both rooms. Twin beds were set up in each, cheerfully made up in red and green plaids. Her bags were set up on one of them. Her siblings had already laid claim to their room, Ginny scattering stuffed animals—far more than she'd had packed when Tara left her—and Austin his art supplies and comic books.

"Well, I guess they've made themselves right at home."

A chuckle rumbled in Jace's chest. "They're great."

She sighed and turned toward him, suddenly finding herself at eye level with his mouth. Because she wanted to stare at it, Tara forced her eyes upward. His cheeks were ruddy from the cold and he smelled of evergreens. She had the ridiculous desire to lean in for a better sniff, wanting to stroke her hand along the five o'clock shadow that darkened his cheeks.

Idiot. She wasn't in a position to be noticing the fact that he was incredibly attractive. She had far too many responsibilities for that.

"So, um, where are the little heathens?"

"In the kitchen with Mom, baking cookies."

"Cookies?" Tara couldn't keep the alarm out of her voice. "Ginny's diabetic. Has she been eating the—"

"Sugar free cookies," Jace assured her. "Austin's keeping an eagle eye on her. He warned us before we got started."

Tara exhaled slowly, willing her heartbeat to slow. "Sorry. We had an ER trip last year with a massive hyperglycemic attack. I guess I'm still not over it."

"It's fine. I don't expect that's the kind of scare you ever really get over."

True enough.

"So it's just you? Nobody to pitch in with them?"

She shot a glare his way. "You've been coming into The Grind almost every day and flirting for the past two weeks. I don't for a second believe you haven't been asking around about me."

"I'm not interested in gossip. I'm asking you."

Not an outright denial. Tara didn't know if she preferred his direct approach or not.

Well, she wanted to put some distance between them. This had certainly worked with anyone else who'd tried to get too close.

"Our father is in prison. Burglary. He had primary custody of the kids at the time of his arrest. Their mother disappeared for parts unknown years ago. Dad's parents are dead and I don't know about the kids' maternal grandparents. As far as anybody knows, I am the only family they have left, so I've basically been a mom since I was nineteen. It's me or the foster system, and I won't do anything to jeopardize that."

Jace didn't look put off at all. In fact he looked...impressed? "You're doing a great job with them."

That's exactly what she *didn't* know. Giving

into a rare burst of agitation, Tara paced away, toward the tree. "You haven't been around them enough to know that." She turned to pace back, only to realize he'd followed and she smacked right into his chest.

Jace reached up reflexively to steady her, and those big, broad hands curved around her shoulders. "I've been around them enough to know that Ginny thinks you walk on water and Austin respects you."

"My brother doesn't respect me. He barely even tolerates me." Tara's hand splayed across his chest against the navy sweater. She forgot what she'd said. Why wasn't Jace letting her go? Why wasn't she pushing him away?

"Maybe he didn't at first. But you've proved you'll stick. You give him rules and boundaries —which he needs—and every single day, you prove you care. And if he's said otherwise to your face, well, he's eleven. All little boys are punk ass kids at eleven."

Tara's lips twitched. "Were you?" She could

imagine a smaller version of him, same impish grin, same big brown eyes feigning innocence.

"Me? Oh no. Livia was the punk ass. I was a sainted angel. And if my mother tells you otherwise, she's lying."

That wrangled a chuckle out of her. "Your halo's a little crooked there, Jace."

He released her and reached up, miming straightening the thing. "Better?"

She'd felt better with his hands on her. Grounded. The way she'd once felt with good dance partners, when she knew she could leap for the sky and they would catch her. Tara decided not to give too much thought to that. "Might need some spit and polish. Meanwhile, I should round up the kids and sort out dinner."

"Should be ready any minute. C'mon." He headed for the door.

"Y'all don't have to feed us," Tara protested, then belatedly wondered if he'd brought the contents of the fridge as well as the tree.

"You just moved in. Nobody expected you to cook. And around here, everybody takes a turn at KP. You'll get yours. Livia's on deck tonight, and I heard rumors of pork loin and roasted vegetables. After that, carols by the fire."

"Seriously?" she asked, following him down the stairs.

"We take Christmas very seriously around here."

I'm dreaming. I'm dreaming and I'm trapped in a Hallmark Channel Christmas movie.

"Well. Okay then." What else was there to say?

MUSIC SPILLED out the moment Jace opened the door to the main house. The cheerful strings of *The Nutcracker,* at a guess. Beside him, Tara flinched.

Not a classical music fan? He recalled this had been playing the last several times he'd been in The Grind. Maybe she'd ODed.

Ginny's giggles carried from the living room.

"We're ready," his mother declared.

The little girl stood in front of the fireplace, in a space vacated by the coffee table. Jace's parents and sister sat lined up in a row on the sofa, a willing audience. Ginny's shoes were off, her hands held in some dancer's pose as her head bobbed in time with the music, counting in. The moment she spied her sister, she broke form and raced over.

"Tara! Listen! It's the 'Waltz of the Snowflakes'! Dance with me." She dragged at Tara's hands, pulling her into the room.

"I don't think there's time before dinner, munchkin." Her voice came out normal, but Jace could see the tension in her shoulders.

"Oh everything's on warm in the oven and the bread needs to cool before we slice it," Livia said. "Besides, there's always time for performing. Isn't that right, Ginny?"

"Yeah! Please, Tara? Please please please please?"

From his position slouched in a chair, Austin rolled his eyes.

Tara looked down at her sister, obviously searching for the right thing to say. She didn't want to dance. Not in front of all of them. That much was obvious. Being goofy at home with your kid sister was a lot different from being goofy in front of relative strangers.

Jace stepped forward, intending to rescue her, but as it turned out, Tara couldn't deny her baby sister anything.

"All right. But just one. I'm starving." Tara moved to toe off her shoes and shrug out of her coat. "You may want to push the furniture back a little. My legs are longer than Ginny's."

By the time they'd shoved the sofa and chairs further back, the music had shifted yet again.

"Do you want to go back to the 'Waltz of the Snowflakes'?" she asked Ginny.

"The 'Spanish Dance' will do," Ginny said, quite seriously.

Jace perched on the arm of Austin's chair and settled in to watch as the sisters took their positions. Ginny looked over, tried to match her stance to Tara's. Some formal pose with their arms curved and their feet in opposite L shapes. It was going to be fun to see Tara loosen up.

Then the music started and they began to dance, mirroring each other in posturing bows to their tiny crowd. Whatever assumptions he'd made that they'd be silly or awkward vanished the moment Tara began to move. Her arms reached for the sky in long, graceful lines. As a unit, she and Ginny took several steps to the side, reaching and pointing. Tara's leg snapped up, high as her head with each pass. As the music escalated, the pair of them spun in circles Jace thought of as more common on ice skates. But Tara did it without any apparent effort. Jesus, how could anyone actually balance on their toes like that? What kind of strength must be in those feet?

Coming out of a spin, Ginny lost her balance with a giggle, landing splayed in Livia's lap. Tara kept going. Jace realized her eyes were closed and half expected her to run into someone or something. But she never faltered, moving in perfect tune with the music until it came to a close, her body bent in a graceful arc, one foot curved impossibly above her head. Her expression when she stopped was caught somewhere between pleasure and pain. She held the position until the next track began, then unfolded in a sinuous motion entirely in keeping with the 'Arabian Dance' that was starting. Jace didn't even think she was aware of doing it.

He was the first to break the stunned silence. "I think I speak for all of us when I say, wow. I had no idea you were a dancer."

The openness in her face shifted to something else, a flash of pain quickly shuttered by her usual even expression. "I'm not."

"Pretty sure everything we just saw points to the contrary," Livia said.

"I *was* a dancer." Her tone indicated the subject was closed. She bent to tug on her shoes. "Now, time for you both to wash your hands for supper."

The kids raced down the hall to do as she asked.

Dinner was a raucous affair, with Ginny and Austin providing a play-by-play of their evening since they arrived at the farm.

"—and then we met Kip. He likes to play fetch and give kisses," Ginny reported. "I wanted to bring him to my room, but Jace said he sleeps in the barn."

"He does," Jace's dad, Evan, said. "He's a total bed hog otherwise."

"I'm tiny. I don't mind."

"Yeah but if we let him sleep with you, it'd spoil him and then he'd expect to come inside all the time," Linda told her.

"Plus he keeps Pepper company so she doesn't have bad dreams," Jace said.

Ginny looked worried. "Pepper has bad dreams?"

Uh oh. Misstep.

"Not with Kip," he assured her. "They snuggle up in her stall."

"I have bad dreams sometimes," the little girl said quietly.

"And you can come crawl into bed with me if you do. I'm right across the hall," Tara said. "But after the day you've had I'm sure visions of puppies and Christmas trees will be dancing in your little head."

"And sugar plums!"

"What is a sugar plum anyway?" Jace wondered. "It always sounded like a fruit snack."

"Maybe we'll look it up on Google and see if we can make some, while you're here," Linda said.

They all cleared the table.

"How about you two come with me and run off some energy before bed," Evan suggested.

"Oh, I don't want to put you out," Tara said. "I'm sure you have something you'd rather be doing."

"Not a thing. C'mon kids!"

Linda laid a hand on her shoulder. "They're a real pleasure to have around. If it's okay with you, I'd really love to adopt Ginny and Austin as my grands for the holiday since my two haven't seen fit to grace me with any yet."

"Still finishing school," Jace protested.

"Still single," Livia answered.

"Yeah, yeah. I know. But I'm not getting any younger!"

"I—well that's lovely, thank you, Mrs. Applewhite."

"Please, call me Linda."

After finishing up the dishes, Jace wandered outside in search of Tara.

She stood at the porch rail, watching them running and shrieking with laughter in the lights from the barn. "I don't think I've ever heard them this happy."

Jace propped himself on a column beside her, wishing *she* looked happy. "It's a simple enough thing."

She turned to him. "But it's not. I don't know how to thank you for this. I mean, you don't even know us and you've brought all of us out here, more or less into your home, for a holiday that's meant for family." Her posture was stiff as her voice, and flags of color burned in her cheeks.

"That was an easy thing, too. We have plenty of room."

"And that's it? You have room, you saw a need, so boom, you just finagle complete strangers into coming to your home?"

Her look of total consternation made him smile. "You're still mad I wrangled you into this."

"Oh, we're going to put that out in the open? Fine. Yes, I am. I don't like being maneuvered. I especially don't like my siblings being used for manipulation. But you set it up in such a way that I couldn't say no without destroying Christmas for them."

That wiped the smile off his face. "That wasn't my intention. Truly, it wasn't."

"Then what was your intention, Jace? Why are you doing this? What do you hope to get out of it?"

He thought of the sadness that lurked in her eyes and that need he had to do something about it for her as he hadn't been able to for someone else. "A smile."

Tara shook her head. "What?"

"If all goes according to plan, I hope to get a smile out of it."

"A smile?" At another hoot of laugher, she shot a glance into the yard, making sure the kids were okay. "From the kids?"

"From you. I'm betting yours is killer."

Tara obviously had no idea what to say to that.

Because he couldn't help himself, Jace reached out to tuck a lock of hair behind her ear. "You have the prettiest, saddest eyes, I've ever seen."

She frowned. "So—what? You decided to play Santa to me and my family to fix it?"

"I'm not arrogant enough to believe I can fix it." He'd learned that hard lesson well enough with Jordan. "But getting a real smile out of you is the kind of personal challenge I like."

"Look, Jace. You're a nice guy. Obviously you are. And I can appreciate that you're apparently interested in me, but I just can't—I'm not in a position to think about something so simple as dating. I've got too much respon- sibility."

Unperturbed, he nodded. "I respect that. But for while you're staying at the farm, you've got help. People who legitimately dig the kids and want to spend time with them. I swear to you they aren't a burden. So maybe for however long you're here, you could give yourself a break and enjoy a good, old fashioned country Christmas."

Tara frowned. "No strings?"

"No strings," he assured her.

She shook her head. "I don't understand you."

"Do you need to?"

"I need things to make sense. Generally when something seems too good to be true, it is. Everything you're offering here seems like it should have a gigantic neon sign blinking Suckers Apply Here."

Jace could've been offended at that. But that

kind of attitude didn't develop without having learned some hard lessons. So instead he said, "You know what the best part of a good, old-fashioned country Christmas is?"

"What?"

"The more the merrier. If there's one thing that Applewhites know, it's how to do Christmas. We want to do this for you, for your brother and sister. Because we can. Because it's fun. And yeah, I am interested in more than that—not gonna lie—but I'm not going to push you. So just take what I'm offering here and enjoy it. I get the sense you haven't let yourself do that since you took charge of the kids."

She gave a soft, self-deprecatory laugh. "That's true enough. So I'll stop being rude and looking this gift horse in the mouth and just say thank you for your hospitality."

That, Jace decided, was a start.

CHAPTER 5

"I HAVE THE PRETTIEST, saddest eyes he's ever seen? I mean, what the heck am I supposed to say to that?" Tara demanded.

Daniel, the other barista on duty, listened with rapt attention. "Did he touch you as he said it?"

She pretended she had to think about it, though the gesture was burned into her brain. "He tucked my hair behind my ear."

"That's so romantic," he sighed, absently

placing the pre-filled coffee filter into the waiting container.

"Focus, Daniel. He thinks I'm sad."

He unfolded the next filter and held it waiting for the fresh ground beans Tara was scooping. "Honey, you are sad."

"Seriously? Is this what people see when they look at me?" More importantly, is this what her brother and sister saw? The last thing she wanted was for either of them to feel like she resented them for what she had to give up to take care of them.

"Probably not most people. Most folks don't look too close. But sweetheart, you've got cocker spaniel eyes. Big and soulful. And yes, sad. But who can blame you? You were basically a mom at nineteen. While everybody else is out doing the college thing, you're here earning your angel wings. It's noble and honorable, but you wouldn't be human if that didn't make you sad sometimes."

"Then I suppose I'm very human." She finished with the Anjilinaka from Bolivia and moved on to the Riakiberu from Kenya. "I don't regret it. If I had it to do over, I'd do the exact same thing. I just...I guess I'm feeling what I gave up a little more keenly right now."

As if on cue, "The Waltz of the Flowers" began to play on their internet radio station. Again.

Right. Twist that knife a little deeper.

"Sounds like your Mr. Applewhite wants to make up for that."

"He's not mine."

"Well, clearly he wants to be."

Tara fisted both hands on her hips. "I don't get it. Why? What's in this for him? He doesn't know me. Yet he's going out of his way to be nice to me, to my brother and sister. Nobody does all that for just a smile."

"A smile?"

"That's what he said he was after when I asked him. He wanted to make me smile."

"Oh honey." Daniel laid a hand over his heart. "That is just the sweetest—"

"Craziest," Tara interrupted.

"You, my darling girl, are jaded and suspicious."

"I have to be jaded and suspicious. The world is not a nice place, Daniel."

"You don't live in the world, sweet cheeks. You live in Wishful."

"Which, I concede is a nicer place than most, but still."

"I think you're looking for some ulterior motive where there is none. You need to consider the fact this really is what it appears to be."

"Which is?"

"You've caught the attention of a real dreamboat guy, and he just wants to spend time with you. And, in this case, I don't mean 'spend time' as a euphemism. Although Jace Applewhite is hunky and delicious enough that if I weren't with Christoff and he swung the other way, I'd be all about spending some quality time with him."

"Daniel," she chided.

"What? Don't you find him attractive?"

"If you like the tall, broad-shouldered lumberjack type." She pictured Jace hefting that axe. "With those big, capable hands..."

Daniel grinned.

"Okay, yes, damn it, I find him attractive. I'm not blind or dead." Which was probably part of the problem. It wasn't nearly as easy to shut off the attraction to Jace as it had been to the various other guys who'd shown interest over the last year and a half.

"So what's stopping you?"

"I don't have time for dating." She'd made the excuse often enough, it fell off her tongue in a rote recitation. "I am, as you pointed out, basically a mom. A single mom at that."

Daniel took her by the shoulders. "Sweetie, I respect the fact that you've embraced that role and all the responsibilities that go with it. God knows those kids needed that. But it's still important for you to remember that you're more than that."

How can I be, when I'm here? In coming to Wishful to be guardian to her siblings, she'd given up the core of her identity. "I barely remember what else I am or used to be."

"You are a vibrant and gorgeous woman in her prime, who deserves to get a little attention just for her. Jace Applewhite wants to give you that attention. And he's arranged for a situation where you actually have opportunity for that. Why on earth wouldn't you take advantage of that?"

"Because." There were reasons.

"Because, why?"

"I don't know if I even remember how."

"How long has it been since you did something as normal as going out on a date?"

"A year. And I'm not sure it actually counts as a date. When he came to pick me up at the house and saw the kids and babysitter, it took him only about twenty minutes to make his excuses and drop me back off. Nobody in my age bracket wants to sign on for a package deal. And who can blame them? Twenty-one is hardly the time most people are thinking about kids. They're too busy figuring out what they want to do with their lives, playing the field. Nobody wants to be a pseudo-parent at that age." God knew she hadn't.

"Yes, but consider the fact that Jace knows about the kids. Knew about them when he offered up the apartment. He's known about them all along and seems to enjoy spending actual time with them. All points in his favor. He's still not running. He actually likes you, Tara."

He hadn't balked at the news that her father was in prison either.

"You think I should give him a chance."

"I think you should give yourself a chance. Take this opportunity to be a normal girl for once."

Tara thought of the wish she'd made a couple of weeks before. Was that what this was? The unexpected answer to her first wish? If that were the case, it was probably bad luck not to accept it. Right?

"Well...what harm could it do?"

"You want to slide your hand through here like this and then just rub the comb in circles." Jace demonstrated the curry comb on Pepper's flank.

Ginny looked doubtful. "But it's all pokey. Doesn't it hurt?"

"Nope. See, she likes it. It's like getting a massage. Just be sure not to use it on her legs or head."

"I can do that."

Jace helped her onto a stool so she'd be at the right height and handed over the comb. "That's it, you've got it."

He moved over to check on Austin. "How you coming with Rupert?"

"Pretty good."

Satisfied the kids were occupied, Jace took a seat and began polishing up the wagon harnesses. Ginny kept up a steady commentary talking to Pepper, giving a repeat of the same play-by-play she'd given him when he'd picked them up from school. Her brother stayed silent, only occasionally murmuring to the gelding.

The boy had a good hand with the horses. Calm and gentle. They were good kids.

As he dipped his polishing cloth into the saddle soap, Jace realized Austin was studying him.

"Something on your mind?"

"Are you a player?"

"Sports or video games?" If the kid was into football, he totally had the latest Madden on Xbox. Or they could pull out the actual ball and toss it around.

"No, I mean, are you serious about my sister or just messing with her?"

Oh. Jace looked up from the harness. Never in his life would he have imagined he'd be having the "what are your intentions?" talk with a fifth grader.

"I am absolutely, a hundred percent not messing with Tara. I wouldn't do that to her. I like her. We're friends. Or working on it."

Austin wasn't buying it. "Friends isn't what you're going for."

Astute kid. "Honestly, no. I'd like to be more

than friends. But that's entirely up to your sister. Your being here hasn't got anything to do with her decision either way. I want all of you to feel welcome and have fun for the holiday."

"I'm having fun!" Ginny chirped.

Jace smiled. "I'm glad." Looking back at Austin he asked, "Are we cool?"

Another long Look. "Yeah."

"It's good of you to look out for Tara." Jace wondered what she'd say if she knew her baby brother was as protective of her as she was of him.

"She looks out for us. Somebody ought to be looking out for her."

"Tara's the best sister in the whole, wide world," Ginny declared.

"I happen to think she's pretty awesome, too," Jace told her.

"She stayed," Austin said simply. "She stayed when she didn't have to. A lot of people wouldn't."

Jace could hear what he wasn't saying. That a lot of people hadn't.

"She loves you."

"I wish we could do something for her, but we don't have anything to spend."

Jace realized they must be on an exceptionally tight budget with Tara supporting all of them on her wages as a barista and the money from her yoga classes. It said a lot that she was pulling it off. "What if we could do something about that?"

"How's that?"

No donations here. Austin's tone made it clear he wouldn't accept charity any more than Tara would.

"Y'all made most of the ornaments on your tree, right?"

"Yeah. Tara taught us how to make several last Christmas."

"Austin did the painted balls," Ginny announced proudly.

"Yeah?" Their tree boasted a dozen balls with tiny holiday scenes painstakingly painted on each. "You're really talented."

The boy just jerked his shoulders.

"You could make more and sell them. We get a surprising amount of traffic between now and Christmas. People buying last minute trees or fresh wreaths or garland. Those ornaments would make great last minute gifts or impulse buys."

"We don't have supplies."

Jace waved that off. "We can pick some up. The cost of supplies will come out of the profits and anything over that is gravy."

Ginny bounced on her stool. "Let's do it, Austin. It'll be fun!"

"How long do you think it would take you to make some?" Jace asked.

"A few hours per batch. Mostly letting glue or paint dry."

"If y'all can make me a list of what you need, I can make a supply run while you're in school tomorrow and you can dive in when you get home."

"My brushes and stuff are still at the house."

"I can swing by and get those, too."

"But how will we keep it a surprise?" Ginny wanted to know.

"We'll set up in the big house. There's plenty of space and rooms Tara won't go in."

Austin and Ginny peered around the horses and exchanged a look. "Sounds like a plan," he said.

"What's a plan?" Tara asked, walking into the barn.

The kids jolted guiltily and Jace raced to cover. "The kids want to learn how to make wreaths out of the tree trimmings. I told them we'd have a little wreath-making class on Saturday and they can help me finish up the last batch we'll be taking in to sell at Edison Hardware."

"Count me in to help with that," she said.

"Yeah?"

"It's the least we can do to say thank you for your hospitality." She lifted a caddy of drinks. "I brought treats from The Grind. Hot chocolate with whipped cream for you two."

"Awesome!"

"Yay!"

She handed over the cups to her siblings. "And your mocha with a shot of caramel."

Jace grinned, delighted she'd remembered. "I told you I'd be a regular before you knew it. Thanks." He sipped at the drink and found it perfect.

"So, what are we doing here?"

"Playing horse salon," Ginny told her.

"They're grooming; I'm polishing."

"Sounds productive. Think you'll still have energy after dinner to make cookies for teacher gifts? Miss Linda said we can take over the kitchen in the big house after supper."

"Did you get sprinkles?" Ginny asked.

"I did. And the stuff to make icing."

"Cookies are good," Austin said.

"Yes they are. I'm going to go mix up the dough and get it chilling so that we're all set to roll out and bake after supper." She paused on her way out and looked back at Jace, a tentative curve to her lips. "Maybe if you're not busy, you'd like to help? We eat the disasters."

"What she means is we make disasters on purpose so we have some to eat," Austin corrected.

Another step in the right direction. "I'd love to help make disasters."

Tara nodded. "Then I'll see you in the kitchen."

CHAPTER 6

"INCOMING HOTTIE ALERT."

AT Daniel's warning, Tara looked up to see Jace coming through the door of The Grind. Her mood lifted at the sight of him even before she took in the striped hat with elf ears. When was the last time she'd been this happy to see someone?

His mom came in on his heels, a Santa hat perched in her silvering blonde hair.

"Well don't you two look festive?" Tara said.

"It's the only time of year I can display my ears without ridicule," Jace deadpanned.

Tara chuckled.

"We've been Christmas shopping," Linda said.

"Ugh, I am so behind on that," Tara admitted. "I just haven't had time to go."

"You should come with us," Jace suggested. "You're off in a little bit, right?"

"I am, but I have to go pick up the kids from school. It's their last day, so they're going to be wild."

"Oh, let me get them," Linda said. "I found a recipe for those sugar plums we talked about and got all the stuff to make them. And they have such fun helping in the kitchen."

"Making a mess in the kitchen, you mean."

Linda waved that off. "It's just part of the process. Seriously, though, I'd love to keep them. And I was a nurse before I retired, so I can handle Ginny's insulin when it's necessary. You go shopping with Jace. It'll save you from being part of the very last minute crowd."

"You're sure you don't mind?"

"Not at all. They're a delight."

"Plus I need to ditch her so I can go buy her present in secret," Jace said.

"Well, if you're really sure."

"It's settled then. I'll get the kids and you two can go do your top secret shopping. You might as well head to Lawley and make an evening of it. More shopping options there."

And so it was Tara found herself pulling onto the highway a half hour later, with Jace in the passenger seat.

"I see where you get it," she said.

"Get what?"

"Your ability to sweetly railroad people. You and your mother are like a couple of border collies. Herding people where you want them to go."

Jace laughed. "I'll take that as a compliment."

"She totally set me up." Tara cut her eyes in his direction. "Or was it your idea?"

"She likes you. And she knows I like you. So make of that what you will."

Rather than being uncomfortable, Tara felt kind of warm and fuzzy about the whole thing.

She got to spend the next few hours with an attentive, attractive guy, without worrying about her siblings. She'd had no idea how good that would feel.

"So do you have a list?" she asked.

"Nope. Finished my shopping last week."

"Seriously?"

"Online shopping baby. They deliver stuff right to your door. But I'm still on the hunt for stocking stuffers. Where all do you need to go?"

"I'm not sure, exactly. I haven't quite adjusted to not having access to everything in the Dallas metro area."

"Dallas? Is that where you're from originally?"

"Originally, no. I grew up in Jackson. But I was in college at SMU before I came here."

"Yeah? What were you studying?"

Tara hesitated. But this was a logical part of that get to know each other routine. There was no sense in hiding it from him. "Dance. I was working on my BFA in dance performance. SMU has one of the top programs in the country." She paused. "You're the first person I've told that to in Wishful."

"Really? Why?"

"Why do I keep it quiet or why did I decide to tell you?"

"Both."

"I started ballet when I was four, and I loved it. I knew from the first time I successfully did a pirouette that I didn't want to do anything else. And as it happens, I had enough of an aptitude that I could pursue it professionally. That was the plan, anyway.

"I was in the middle of my sophomore year when my father was arrested and the social worker tracked me down. I'd never even met Ginny and Austin, and I'd just been cast as Sugar Plum Fairy for that year's production of *The Nutcracker*, which was an enormous honor. Underclassmen never get cast in the principal roles."

"You came anyway."

"I came anyway. And they gave the role to someone else."

"So that's why Christmas makes you sad. Because Christmas means *The Nutcracker* and the role you gave up."

"It's brutal. It plays everywhere from Thanksgiving to New Year's."

"That's rough. But you'll go back someday."

The knife in her heart twisted a little deeper. "I won't get the chance. The kids need me, and by the time they're old enough to be out on their own, I'll be too old to go back."

She could feel him watching her. "You knew that when you came here, didn't you?"

The lump in her throat kept her from speaking, so she nodded.

"You walked away from your dream to give your siblings a better life." When she said nothing he continued, "That must've been really hard."

Tara couldn't keep the bitterness from her voice. "What do you want me to say? That it was like losing a limb? Cutting out my heart? It was. It's the hardest thing I've ever done. But it wasn't a choice. Not for me."

"That says a lot about the kind of person you are."

She shrugged, uncomfortable with the admiration in his tone. "My mother doesn't understand it. As far as she's concerned, I took all the years of training, all the classes and work and advantages she worked to give me and threw it all away on kids I didn't even know, who, in her eyes, had no connection to me."

"She's still got issues with your dad, I take it."

"He was a mistake. One she spent my entire life trying to distance us from. So she sees the fact that I'm here, that I've taken primary custody of my half-siblings, as a slap in the face and a rejection. Like I somehow chose him over her."

"You aren't here for him."

That he saw that, understood it, soothed something in her.

"You're right. I'm not. My dad is a screw up, and I'm not going to let Austin and Ginny pay for his mistakes." Realizing her hands were fisted around the steering wheel, she made a conscious effort to relax. "I miss dance. And I'm probably still working my way through the stages of grief about the fact that I'm not going to get to pursue it as a career. But I don't regret walking away for them. I don't talk about it because I'm just not where I can yet without feeling like I've been gutted, and I don't ever want them to feel like I resent them for being the reason I gave it up."

"For what it's worth, I don't think either of them thinks that." He went quiet for a moment. "What about the rest? Why tell me?"

Tara looked over and met his eyes. "Because you're the first guy who found out about my situation who didn't look at me with scorn or pity."

"What kind of assholes have you been hanging out with?"

She laughed. "None. None at all."

"I don't see anything to pity in your situation. I see plenty to admire. You've done a good job with them under difficult circumstances.

And maybe you don't want praise or recognition for that, but you deserve it either way."

"I'm not looking for a reward. I just want to do right by them. And right now I want to give them the best Christmas I possibly can."

NOW THAT SHE'D pointed it out, Jace noticed strains of *The Nutcracker* absolutely everywhere they went. As she went about picking the perfect gifts for her siblings, Tara didn't seem quite as weighed down as she had, but her story bugged him. Talent like that shouldn't be wasted. Her situation wasn't the same as Jordan's, but he could see just as much futility. It wasn't like Wishful was exactly a hotbed of culture. Still, there had to be something to be done.

"Oh my God, this is perfect."

Jace dialed his attention back in time to see Tara running her hands over a...what the heck was that? Three tiers of purple and pink, with lots of glitter and some kind of sloping roof, it was clearly girly. "Is that a princess tower doll-house thing?"

"It's a princess tower bookcase. Ginny adores books. Right now we've got a stack of milk crates to hold her collection, but this would be so cute in her room. I'm buying it."

"Your wish, milady." Jace reached out and hefted it into the basket. "What about Austin?"

"I want to find him a drafting table. I got an easel for his birthday, but he's really more into drawing."

They wandered the aisles. Jace snuck in some sketch pads and a set of charcoal pencils.

"What are you doing?" Tara asked.

"I told you. Stocking stuffers."

Panic flitted over her face. "I don't think the kids actually have stockings. I never found them last year and I didn't even think—"

"Relax. Mom has it covered. Didn't you see them hanging from the mantle after dinner last night?" There was one with her name embroidered on it, too.

Her lips pressed into a line, but he could see the amusement in her eyes. "I was way more concerned with cleaning the icing off the ceiling. I should've made you do that. You were the one who started that war."

Jace didn't even bother to snuff the grin. "How was I supposed to know his aim would be lousy?"

"I think it was less the aim and more his ammunition of choice."

"At least you hadn't tinted it yet."

"Small mercies. Oh, this is it. This is what I want for him." She circled around a display model drafting table, complete with little containers and trays to corral pencils and erasers and whatever other art supplies Austin might use.

They hunted up one still in the box.

"I think that's it," Tara declared.

"Not quite. I saw something earlier I decided I want to nab." Jace navigated back through the aisles until he found what he was looking for.

"Model horses?" she asked.

"I thought Ginny would dig them." He picked up the two that looked most like Pepper and Rupert.

"Which one of us are you trying to woo? Her or me?"

"Bonus points if it helps with both."

"You're incorrigible. But charming."

Jace perked up. "You find me charming?"

"Against my better judgment."

"Excellent." He rubbed his hands together and drew his brows down in his best evil mastermind impression. "Then it's only a matter of time before I wear you down."

"I'm not sure how I feel about that tactic. It doesn't exactly scream romance."

Jace stopped in the middle of the aisle. "I can do romance. I've been dying to do romance. But I wanted to respect your wishes. Is that a green light?"

She hesitated. "I think maybe it is."

"You're not sure?"

"I'm not sure of much of anything these

days. But you've heard all about how complicated my life is and you're not running. That's…beyond refreshing. You've given me a chance, so it seems only fair that I give you one."

"I can work with that." He restrained himself from leaping into the air with a whoop and settled for tucking her arm through his. "Let's go check out."

Over a quick dinner of Mexican food, they decided to swing by her house to wrap the gifts before heading back to the farm.

As they hauled the pile inside, Jace was forced to admit that maybe they'd gone a little bit overboard. And she didn't even know about the stuff he and his mom had bought earlier in the day. But damn, it was fun to shop for kids!

"Are you going to leave everything here until Christmas Eve or do you want to find somewhere to hide them at the farm?"

Tara didn't answer. She stood, frowning, in the middle of the living room.

"What is it?"

"It's warm."

"Well, it's out of the wind and—"

"No, it's actually warm. The heat's running."

"Oh." And that thought made him go cold. "Are you sure?"

She headed into the kitchen and switched on one of the burners. With a small hiss and a click, the flame lit. "The gas is back on."

"Are you sure there wasn't some just left over in the lines?" Maybe it was selfish, but he didn't want the gas lines fixed. He didn't want her to have the option to leave the farm. Not yet.

They got their answer via a flier stuffed in the mailbox. Notice from the gas company that the breach had been repaired and all was well just in time for Christmas.

"We can come home." She sounded less enthusiastic about that prospect than she would've a week ago. That gave him hope.

"Don't."

"Jace— "

He could see that sense of responsibility

creeping back and scrambled to head it off. "You're all settled in at the farm. The kids are having fun. My parents are having a ball spoiling them silly. Stay and finish out that country Christmas I promised you." He took her hand and pressed it to his heart. "Stay and see where this goes."

CHAPTER 7

*H*E'D BE GOING BACK to school soon. What could really come of the next few days? A part of her wanted to just walk away, get back to her normal life, where everything made sense, where she was in control. But a bigger part looked into his earnest face, into those big brown eyes and wanted to stay in the fantasy he'd created. Even knowing it would end—had to end—she wanted those days with him. Wanted to take the time to pretend that she was just a girl who had the luxury of being courted by a sweet, handsome guy.

What harm could it do?

"Seems a shame to miss out on the chance of having a white Christmas out at the farm."

"That it does." He lifted the hand he still held and pressed a kiss to her knuckles.

The gesture made her knees go weak. She'd given him the green light to romance her. As a start, she absolutely couldn't fault this. Anticipatory nerves sparked, and Tara felt herself sway toward him, wishing he'd put those lips to better use.

But he didn't press his advantage. With one last stroke of his thumb that left her palm tingling, he let her go. "Shall we wrap?"

The nerves which had knotted up her belly loosened. "You want ribbon or paper?"

"Paper. My bows look like Kip's chew toys."

"Paper it is, then." Tara gathered up the supplies and brought them into the living room. Despite her vague disappointment, she liked that he didn't push. It'd been so long since she'd played this game, and she'd never played it all that much to begin with. She'd been too focused on her training to spend much time on dating. She wasn't sure of her footing. For a dancer, who always had her balance, that was a rather scary place to be.

Jace kept up a steady banter during their wrapping session, making her laugh by putting bows in his hair. He was easy to be with. Easy to talk to. Just...easy. Tara didn't feel like she needed to be constantly on guard with him. And that made her realize exactly how much she was on guard the rest of the time. The fact that she could relax around him might've been the best gift he could've given her.

She caught herself looking at his mouth.

Then again...

But maybe he was right to hold off and take things really slow. It would hardly do for him to kiss her now, when they'd just decided she'd stay at the farm for the rest of the holiday. What if it was a dud of a kiss? Then things would be all weird. No. Better to ease into this.

The clock was ticking on toward nine by the

time they finished up and headed back out to the farm.

"I absolutely did not mean to abandon your mom with the kids this long."

"She'd have called if she was having problems. She did manage to raise two of us just fine."

"Still."

"Did you have fun today?"

Tara looked over from the driver's seat. "More than I've had in longer than I care to remember."

"Then there's no reason to feel guilty."

"You may sing a different tune if we get back and they're bouncing off the ceiling."

The kids were, in fact, in the middle of a high stakes game of Monopoly with Livia and Evan.

"Ginny's going to bankrupt us all," Livia declared. "Do you have any idea how many times I've landed on Boardwalk? With hotels? I'm in hock up to my eyebrows."

Tara scooped Ginny up and snuggled her

into her lap. "I should've warned you. She's ruthlessly competitive at board games. And she should also be finding a stopping place because it's past her bedtime."

"Aw, but there's no school tomorrow."

Livia rolled the dice and ended up at Park Place. "I fold. I don't feel like going through all the hassle of selling my mortgaged properties back to the bank."

Austin picked up the thick stack of colorful Monopoly money. "I think it's safe to say Ginny won. As usual."

Linda wandered in from the kitchen. "Oh you're back. Did y'all finish your shopping?"

"And wrapping," Tara pronounced. "Thank you for keeping the kids."

"We had a good time. Made up a big batch of sugar plums to pass out as gifts to the rest of the family."

"Did you know they have *twenty-six* people in their family?" Ginny asked.

"Tw—seriously?" Tara waited for somebody to say they were kidding.

"Counting all the cousins, yep. You'll meet most of them at Christmas dinner when we all load up and head to the grandparents'," said Jace. "Everybody within driving distance comes in."

"I'm sorry, you've just boggled my brain. I can't imagine that many people in one family. You have your own football team."

"We have our own version of the Egg Bowl at Thanksgiving," Livia said. "Except instead of the golden egg, we play for Grandma's chess pie. Competition is fierce."

"Since we don't know any of our cousins, Miss Linda says we can borrow theirs this year," Ginny said.

Tara felt a pang. "That's really nice of her. But won't we be intruding?"

"We're an always changing motley crew. Family. Friends. Staff. You won't be the only unfamiliar faces. It's always the more the merrier at the Applewhites," Linda said.

So Jace had told her.

"Well, you just let me know what we can do

to contribute."

"Whatever your best side dish is. There will be an army to feed."

"I can do that." Tara stood. "C'mon, you two. Time to get ready for bed."

Ginny made her rounds, doling out hugs to everyone.

Tara thought back to the shy, wounded child she'd met when she first moved back to Mississippi. Over the last eighteen months, Ginny had blossomed. Even Austin, who trusted so rarely, seemed relaxed and happy, grinning as Livia and Jace ruffled his hair.

This. This was the danger of staying here. They were falling in love with this family. Putting down tender roots that would inevitably be yanked free after the holiday when all the goodwill toward men attitude faded. Not that she thought the Applewhites would ever be deliberately cruel. But taking on three veritable orphans for Christmas was a far cry from keeping them as a permanent part of the family. That kind of transience was exactly why Tara had given up everything to keep Austin and Ginny out of the foster system. Because they needed as much permanence and stability as someone could give them. What would the loss of the Applewhites do to them?

"You're thinking deep thoughts again," Jace said softly.

"Just tired," Tara lied. "It was a full day."

His eyes searched her face and she suspected he saw too much.

"Walk you back?"

She shook her head. "If you come, they'll stay amped up and Ginny will rope you into a bedtime story marathon. We'll see you in the morning."

"Night everybody!" Ginny announced.

Jace scooped her up and gave her a smacking kiss on the cheek. "Good night, Peanut. Don't forget, it's wreath making tomorrow, We'll meet bright and early outside the tree barn after breakfast."

Tara watched the easy way her sister snuggled into him and thought maybe the kids weren't the only ones falling for this family.

"THERE'S SNOW IN THOSE CLOUDS," Tara declared.

Jace followed her gaze to the slate gray sky. "If it happens, it'll be the first white Christmas in seventy-five years. There are pictures of my grandpa as a boy from the last one. He built a snowman as tall as he was. Just over there in front of the house."

"Is he still living?"

"Oh yeah. Fit as a fiddle."

She turned her attention back to the wreath frame, nimbly weaving greenery into the wire. "Why doesn't he live at the farm?"

"Well, it's heavy work. Hard on the body. So Grandma forced him into retirement and my dad took over. Eventually it'll come to me. Well, me and Livia, but I'm much more into the management of the land. That's what I'm in grad school for, actually. Forestry and land management at Mississippi State."

"You're at MSU?"

Jace repressed a smile at her too casual tone. She didn't look up, but her hands paused in the midst of the greenery.

"Yep. Forty-five little minutes away. Easy trip home to see family, friends, or tall, leggy blondes. You know, if that makes a difference."

Ginny pirouetted by, trailing the red ribbon they used for bows. "And you can come home to visit every weekend!"

"I think grad school will keep him a little too busy for that," Tara warned.

"Actually, I've only got one class and thesis hours left, so I only really have to be in Starkville a couple days a week. And I graduate in May. Gotta say, home's looking pretty attractive these days."

A wash of pink crept over Tara's cheeks.

"Oh for the love of Pete, ask the girl out already," Livia said, returning with more wreath frames.

Jace glared at his sister. "I was getting to it."

She rolled her eyes. "Seriously, I'm about to dangle mistletoe from a fishing pole here."

"I saw the rod and reel in the barn," Austin offered.

"Austin!" Tara's blush amped up to match the ribbon, which completely undermined the expression of stern disapproval she aimed his way.

"What?" he shrugged. "I like him. And he checks out."

"He...checks out?" she asked faintly.

"We had a little man-to-man talk and came to an understanding," Jace explained.

"Did you now?"

"Austin *is* the man of the house."

A new respect mingled with the amusement in her eyes as she looked at her brother. "So he is."

"Speaking of which," Jace said. "That other matter we discussed has been taken care of." The kids had picked out a present for Tara. He'd gone ahead and ordered it last night with rush shipping so it would arrive by Christmas Eve. Their ornament sales had more than paid for it, with enough pocket money left over that they could have a little fun of their own.

"Good." Austin nodded in smug satisfaction.

"What are y'all up to?" Tara asked.

"None of your beeswax," Jace told her, sticking his tongue out in his best eleven-year-old fashion.

A mini-van pulled up in front of the barn. A noisy family of four tumbled out, all talking at once as the kids climbed like monkeys up the man who'd been in the driver's seat.

The beaming woman said, "My husband just got back from Afghanistan, so we're a little behind on getting the tree. Can you help us?"

"Certainly. There are plenty left," Jace said. He turned to Austin. "You want to take them out on the wagon?"

"On my own?" His eyes widened.

"You handled things just fine the last half dozen runs with me. I think you're ready."

Austin drew himself up and saluted. "Yes,

sir!"

Laughing, Jace ruffled the boy's hair, and they went to hitch up the horses.

By the time Austin had the horses trotting toward the fields, the family loaded in the back of the wagon, Tara had knocked out another three wreaths. She carried them over to hang on the waiting rack. "You've made his week giving him that responsibility."

"He's good with the horses."

"They've been good for him," said Tara.

"Horses are good therapy."

"So are good people. Your whole family has been good therapy."

Jace leaned back against the work table, crossing his feet at the ankles. "Well, since you're feeling all thankful and sentimental, and my sister has already outed me—"

Livia snorted. "You've been outing yourself for two weeks without our help."

"—I've got tickets to *White Christmas* tonight at the Madrigal. You want to go? Maybe get dinner first?"

"An actual, legitimate date?"

It relieved him that she sounded more amused than anxious. "That would be the general idea."

"Before you answer, it's worth noting that I'm stealing the kids for a Christmas movie marathon. Ginny and Austin don't know who Heat Miser is and this must be rectified," Livia declared.

"In that case, I'd love to."

"Whee!" Ginny launched into another dance, pure joy on her face despite the slight wobble in her balance.

A smile tugged at Tara's lips as she watched, and Jace wanted to see that same look of joy in her eyes.

"Lengthen, Ginny."

Whatever that meant, Ginny did it and her balance settled.

"Is she taking lessons?" Jace asked.

"No. I've been teaching her at home. We couldn't afford formal lessons when I first got here, and the dance studio closed over the summer. I guess there wasn't enough interest to keep it open."

"No, it was because Jeanette had complications from her knee surgery and couldn't teach," Livia said. "She's been in physical therapy for months, but the doctors aren't hopeful."

"How do you even know that?" Jace asked.

"She goes to our church."

"That's tragic." Sympathy twisted Tara's features. "At least I had a choice. Even if I'm not performing anymore, I can still dance."

"So it's not the performance you miss?" Jace asked.

"Don't get me wrong, there's a thrill to the performance, and I love the challenge, but that was never why I did it. Dancing is when I'm most...me, I guess. It's freedom." She gave a self-deprecatory laugh. "That sounds ridiculous."

"Not at all." And it gave him an idea.

He pulled out his phone and sent a text to Leo. *I need a favor.*

CHAPTER 8

TARA FUSSED WITH HER appearance. On any given day, she was far more concerned with getting the kids to school on time and bundling her hair up out of the way for work than she was with impressing anyone. There'd been no one she wanted to impress in longer than she cared to remember. But she wanted to impress Jace. Livia had already taken the kids, so she indulged in all the female date night rituals she'd forsaken for unofficial parenthood, hemming and hawing over the limited wardrobe she'd brought and spending as much time on her hair and makeup as she would've for a professional performance. And maybe this date was a performance, in a way.

Date Night starring Tara Honeycutt as Normal Girl.

A challenging role. Can she pull it off?

His knock came on the apartment door, and she sucked in a bracing breath. She was about to find out.

"It's open!" she called out.

The door opened. "Tara?"

"Be out in a minute. Just putting on my boots." The knee high boots added a couple of inches to her not insignificant height and made her feel strong and sexy.

Jace stood in the living room, hands tucked comfortably in his pockets as he waited, the picture of ease. He turned as she came in and let out a low whistle. "Damn."

And suddenly every minute of fussing was worth it.

Seeming to catch himself, he straightened. "I

hope that doesn't offend you."

To be seen as desirable and, more importantly, as herself? "On the contrary, I find it very...gratifying."

His gaze traveled up from her face to something above her head, his lips twitching. "Someone's been decorating."

"What?"

Tara tipped her own head back to see what he was talking about. Someone had tacked mistletoe to one of the rafters running across the room.

"Austin," she muttered.

"Livia. Or more probably both," Jace said, suddenly three strides closer and beneath the greenery with her.

The boots put her almost eye-level with him, so she could see the twinkle in his eye. "Why do I get the sense you may've had something to do with this?"

"Don't mistake my amusement for involvement. Doesn't mean I don't appreciate the gesture. Are you superstitious, Tara?"

"Most performers are," she allowed.

"It's considered bad luck not to kiss under the mistletoe."

"Well, we certainly wouldn't want any more bad luck." She lifted a hand to his chest, delighted to feel his heart galloping beneath her palm.

Jace slid his hands along her waist, reeling her in until the length of her pressed against the length of him. "I've been thinking about this for weeks," he murmured.

"Then stop thinking." Tara closed the distance between them. She felt his ready smile beneath her lips before he angled his head to take her mouth more firmly.

She lost her balance. She, who could dance her way through a room in the dark, felt her world tilt. Her hands slid up his chest to lock behind his neck, his solid, steady warmth an anchor she was in no hurry to relinquish. His patient, coaxing kiss chased away all the strain, all the nerves, all the worry that shaped her days, leaving nothing behind but a heady sense of being young and alive and wanted.

Jace eased back, pressing his brow to hers. "Well, now I'll be able to concentrate through dinner."

Tara laughed. "Speak for yourself."

One arm still around her waist, he marched her toward the door. "Come on, vixen, let's get some food before my chivalry runs out."

Jace kept his fingers laced with hers on the drive into town. Tara liked how small her hand felt in his. Liked, too, how easy he was with her, despite the attraction simmering between them. By tacit agreement, once they left the farm, neither of them mentioned the kids. Tonight they were just two twenty-somethings out on the town.

Jace was, unsurprisingly, an attentive date. They garnered a few raised eyebrows during their dinner at Speakeasy Pizzeria, a few smiles as they were spotted strolling hand in hand across the town green, walking off the sausage and mushroom pie they'd split before the show. With ample time before curtain, Tara towed him down toward the fountain, despite the frigid air.

The water in the basin was frozen, only the barest of trickles leaking down the center. A scattering of coins lay on the ice, covered in frost.

"Want to make a wish?" he asked.

Tara shook her head. "I already did. A few weeks ago."

"No follow ups?"

Tara slid her arms around his waist in a hug. "No need. You gave me both."

Jace angled his head. "What'd you wish for?"

"I wished that I could give Austin and Ginny the kind of Christmas they deserve. Last year was their first one without Dad. We were still getting to know each other and they were grieving and it was...less than awesome. Raising two kids and an adult on a barista's wages plus a few extras isn't easy. So it was pretty spare, as holidays go. And this year we have you and your amazing family and they're happy—truly happy. I can't repay you for that."

"You don't—"

"I know I don't have to. I know that's not why you did it. But I'm just so grateful you came into our lives." And standing here with his arms around her, it was easier to believe that maybe that wasn't a temporary thing.

"I'm feeling pretty damned lucky myself at the moment. You said both. What was the other wish?"

She ducked her head. "It's stupid."

"You wished it, so it isn't stupid. Tell me."

"I wished that I could be a normal girl. Just for a little while."

"You didn't wish to dance again?"

"That seemed like reaching. And it felt selfish. But the chance to just be normal, without the worries and the burdens. You've gone out of your way to give me that. And it feels wholly inadequate to say thank you—which I know I've already done ad nauseam—but I just...I don't know how to tell you what that means to me. It seems like so much for you to do for only a smile."

Jace tightened his hold on her and rubbed his cold nose against hers. "I *might* have wanted a little more than a smile..."

Laughter burbled up and she brushed a quick kiss against his lips.

"Totally worth it." He reached one hand up, stroking a thumb across her cheek. "No sad eyes."

"Definitely not tonight," she agreed, leaning in to press her cheek to his, chilled skin to chilled skin. "How is it you see what no one else does?"

"Mmm?"

Tara pulled back. "No one else noticed that I was sad. Or if they did, they certainly didn't say anything or try to do something about it. Why did you?"

Something flickered in his face, a mix of regret and memory. "I recognize heartbreak when I see it. And I couldn't, in good conscience, stand by and not try to do something about it. It's sort of my Achilles heel."

"Why?"

"Because you remind me of Jordan."

"And Jordan is…?" *Please don't say a former girlfriend.*

"Jordan Butler. My best friend growing up. You're actually nothing alike on the surface. She's short and dark, brash and reckless. But like you, she found her passion early in life. In her case, it was barrel racing. She was a really gifted rider, wanted to go pro. Probably would have."

"I'm sensing a great big 'but' here."

"Our junior year, she was in a car accident. She was lucky to make it out alive at all. They said it was a miracle she could even walk, but riding was absolutely out of the question. Her leg was too badly damaged."

Tara's heart squeezed. "Oh no. That's terrible."

"Jordan's stubborn. She set out to prove them wrong. Endured countless months of physical therapy. Spent so many hours trying to get back in the saddle. But in the end, the doctors were right. It broke her heart. Her light went out. And nothing I could say or do could make it come back."

"What's she doing now?"

Jace twitched his shoulders. "I don't know. Her family moved while we were in college and we lost touch. I think it was too hard on her to keep up with the people who'd been part of that world with her. I don't guess I ever quite got over not being able to do something to help her, so when I saw that same look in your eyes, I had to try."

Even though she'd been a complete stranger.

God, what a man he was.

Tara framed his face in her hands. "I'm sorry you couldn't help your friend. But I'm grateful you decided to turn that big heart of yours toward helping me."

Jace bowed his head, pressing his brow to

hers. "I'm just glad I had better success." He tipped forward, closing the faint distance between them in a soft, sweet kiss. "Come on. Let's get to the show before we turn into frozen lawn statues for the green."

"But I heard him exclaim as he drove out of sight, 'Merry Christmas to all and to all a good night!'" Jace closed the book and looked up to see Ginny sitting bolt upright in bed, all but bouncing with excitement. He wagged a teasing finger in her direction. "That doesn't look like sleeping all snug in your bed. You know Santa's got radar for stuff like that."

"But I can't sleep! It's Christmas Eve!" she insisted. "And it might snow!"

"I knew we shouldn't have watched all three of *The Santa Clauses*. Drink your Sleepytime tea," Tara said, coming in behind him with two mugs. "If it snows, and I'm awake to see it, I'll wake you up."

Ginny's lower lip poked out as she took her tea.

"Best offer you're gonna get, Peanut," Jace told her.

"Okay," she sulked. "But one more story while we drink tea."

"Which one do you want? And you can't say any of the Harry Potters or Narnia," Tara warned.

"*The Nutcracker*," Ginny said.

"Okay." Tara dug around in the pile of books on the floor before coming up with a slim volume. "Now say good night to Jace."

"Awww, but Jace has to stay and listen tooooooo."

"Jace has to wrap that thing we talked about." He gave her the don't-spoil-the-surprise eyebrow.

Ginny clapped a hand over her mouth.

"You got everything you needed?" Austin asked.

"Yeah, we're good."

Tara looked between the three of them.

"What are you up to?"

"Nothing," they all chorused.

Her face said she wasn't buying it, but she didn't press.

Jace bent to give Ginny a hug and Austin a fist bump. "See y'all in the morning."

"Night, Jace," sang Ginny.

"Night," Austin said.

Jace and Tara exchanged a silent see-you-later look, and he headed back to the house. She'd be coming to join him on wrapping detail once the kids were good and down, but he needed to get a head start on her gift. The whole thing could potentially blow up in his face if he'd read her wrong. But he didn't think he had.

Jace checked his watch. 10:45. Leo would be out to pick up the package in fifteen minutes. Time to get a move on. The bag was in his closet. He checked the contents over, praying Ginny was right when she'd said this was everything Tara would need. Settling all of it into a gift box, he covered the contents in tissue paper and put on the top. The ice skating penguin paper didn't exactly echo the poignancy of the gift, but he'd executed enough low-level spycraft to get this far. He wasn't about to fuss about the wrapping.

Leo pulled up to the front porch steps right as Jace came out, the box in his hands.

"How'd the final show go?"

"Off without a hitch. *White Christmas* is officially wrapped. Since it's Christmas Eve, the post show cast party was possibly the shortest in history. Which is fine. I'm definitely ready to crash."

"Thanks for delaying that for me. Everything set?" Jace asked.

"Yep. It'll be waiting for you tomorrow. Just text me when you're headed into town, and I'll be sure I'm in position. But do me a favor and try to stall and make it after nine so I'm not running out in the middle of Christmas breakfast."

"I'll do my best. We've got kids around this year, so it'll probably be an early morning for us." And Jace found himself a lot more excited by that than he'd expected.

Leo tucked the box into the front seat. "This is either the best Christmas present ever or the worst. I hope it goes the way you want it to, man."

"Me too. Now get on out of here before she sees you."

By the time Tara joined him, Jace was safely back in the living room, surrounded by wrapping supplies. His parents had crashed after the movies, and he'd banished Livia and all her suggestive eyebrow waggles so they'd have some privacy.

"Got them down?"

"Finally. Ginny was in Energizer Bunny mode." She looked around at the assorted gifts from Santa that everyone in his family had felt compelled to pick up. "What is all this?"

"So I wasn't the only one who went a little overboard shopping for the kids. Santa will be well represented."

"Good lord. This is so generous."

"We had a blast." He patted the sofa beside him. "C'mon. Grab some scissors and tape and dive in."

Tara picked her way through the stuff and sank onto the sofa in one of those mindlessly graceful motions that always made him want to stare. "Before we get started, there's something I wanted to give you."

Jace put down his scissors, the better to free up his hands for the expected kiss.

But Tara wasn't leaning in to kiss him. Instead, she pulled something out of her back pocket. "I did some poking around the other night."

"About what?"

"Your friend Jordan."

It was the last thing he'd expected her to say. "Why?"

"Because you aren't the only one susceptible to sad eyes, and it seemed like you've been blaming yourself for not being able to help her all those years ago."

That was true enough.

"Anyway, it's not much, but I thought you might want to know what happened to her."

Jace automatically took the papers she handed him. They felt heavier in his hand than they should. He told himself Tara wouldn't have given them to him if they were bad news. With a bracing breath, he unfolded them. The first page was an engagement announcement. Jordan Marie Butler was scheduled to wed Ezekiel James Wiley, of Bozeman, Montana the coming May.

"She's getting married. Good for her."

"Got married. This was from last year. Look at the second page," Tara prompted.

And there Jordan was, beaming from the saddle. A tall, rangy guy stood beside her, hand draped along the back of the saddle, grin stretched wide as the Rio Grand. The caption of the photo read Snake River Stampede barrel racing champion, Jordan Butler Wiley and her trainer/husband, Zeke Wiley.

"This was six months ago," Tara said.

"She's riding again." Jace ran a finger down

the leg that'd been so mangled in the accident. "She did it. She really did it."

"More to the point, she's happy. Look at her."

There was no denying that. She fairly glowed with it.

Something in Jace loosened, the long-held guilt and worry leeching away. "Good for you, Speedy," he murmured to the picture.

"I bookmarked the link to her Facebook page if you want to try to reconnect."

"I'll do that." Jace set the papers aside and slid his hands into Tara's hair, tugging her in for a kiss. She melted into him and he had to remind himself they were in his parents' living room and had half a toy store to wrap. He eased back before he forgot himself. "Thank you."

"I figured it was the least I could do."

"That's quite a bit more than the least. The least you can do is go on bow duty for all these packages."

"That I can do. Movie accompaniment?"

"How do you feel about *Holiday Inn*?"

"Amenable," she said.

"Then pop it in. We've got a lot of work to do."

CHAPTER 9

CHRISTMAS MORNING BEGAN WITH a snowball fight. Sometime between when she'd stumbled to bed at one and when Ginny woke her at 6:30, three fluffy inches had fallen. Given the rarity of such an event in Mississippi, everybody opted to play first and do presents later. For all they knew, it could disappear by mid-morning. It was all Tara could manage to get the kids into actual clothes under their winter coats instead of their pajamas.

Austin woke Jace with a well-placed snowball to his bedroom window. He rousted everyone else, and the entire Applewhite clan joined in the fun, hair still messy from sleep. While the boys duked it out with freezing ammo, Tara and Ginny made snow angels and started a snowman—though there was only enough snow to manage a small one. Ginny fitted her mittens on the ends of its branch arms and Linda retrieved a carrot for its nose.

"There now, that's a fine snowman," she declared.

"Seems like it should be taller," Ginny said.

Evan looked up at the sky. "Snow's still coming down. There might be enough for a bigger one later."

"Meanwhile, I'm freezing and starving," Livia announced. "Let's get breakfast."

They all tromped, half-soaked, into the big house.

The kids were so excited about the snow, it took them halfway through breakfast to even notice the spread under the big blue spruce in the living room.

"Holy cow!" Her sister gaped. "Tara, do you see all that stuff?"

"I do. Looks like someone was especially good this year."

Ginny bounced in her chair. "Everybody eat fast!"

"Oh, you mean like this?" Jace asked, moving a piece of bacon toward his mouth at a snail's pace.

Ginny darted in and nipped it neatly out of his hand.

"You little imp!"

"You snooze, you lose," she said, without contrition.

Tara all but doubled over with laughter.

"Well, I guess you showed me."

They plowed through bacon, eggs, and biscuits, then the adults took their coffee into the living room.

"I hereby dub Austin the official elf of this morning's festivities." Livia produced the elf hat Jace had worn Christmas shopping and plunked it on Austin's head.

Her brother began passing out gifts. For nearly an hour, they lost themselves in the happy chaos of ripping open paper, and prying open boxes. Ginny tried unsuccessfully to keep hugging the model horses, while opening the rest of her gifts. Austin ended up with a mountain of art supplies to go with his new drafting desk. Linda and Livia ooed and ahed over the custom earring and necklace sets Tara had made them. Jace immediately put on the leather cuff bracelet she'd fashioned to resemble horse tack. All four of the Applewhites proudly put the ornaments the kids had made them on the Christmas tree.

As the pile dwindled, Austin brought one last box over to Tara. "From me and Ginny."

"Oh. Thank you." She ran her hands over the package, wondering what they'd made. It had some pretty serious heft. Tara ripped off the paper to find a magnifying lamp. Definitely not made.

"For your jewelry work," Austin told her.

"We sold ornaments to pay for it," Ginny said proudly.

"And had enough left over for a trip to Chuck E Cheese at some future date," Jace added.

Tara felt her heart swell, both that her siblings had thought of this and that Jace had helped make it happen. She tugged both of them in for a hard hug. "Thank you, both."

"Looks like that's everything," Austin said.

"Nope, there's one more for Tara," Jace announced.

Everybody looked reflexively under the tree, but the space around it was empty.

"We have to go into town to get it."

"Town? But it's Christmas morning. Nothing's open," she said.

"This will be."

Tara narrowed her eyes at him. "What are you up to?"

"A surprise. Everybody load up."

So they did, piling into two cars and caravaning into Wishful. She'd thought maybe he'd done something at the house, but Jace drove them into town proper, down Front Street and turning onto Broad. When he parked in front of The Madrigal Theater, she frowned. "Did you leave something here the other night?"

"Just wait."

Everybody else spilled out onto the sidewalk.

The lobby doors were open. Jace ushered her into the quiet hush and pulled open the door to the auditorium.

"After you," he said.

Tara stepped into the theater and stopped almost at once. A single spotlight was trained on the stage, illuminating a package. In the shadows beyond its glow, she could see that the set from the final scene of White Christmas was still in place.

Jace took her hand and led her down the aisle and up the steps onto the stage. "Go ahead."

After a moment's hesitation, she stepped into the light, feeling her pulse trip as she picked up the box. Her hands shook as she tore the paper and slid her finger under the tape.

"Here, let me help." Jace held the box so she could open the top.

Nestled in the tissue paper were her pointe shoes, the pale pink satin gleaming in the spotlight. Beneath them, some of her dance clothes were neatly folded. "You've been in my closet." It was the only thing she could think to say.

"More properly Ginny has been in your closet. It was a necessary evil for the rest."

"Jace, what's going on?"

"You never got to take the stage as the Sugar Plum Fairy. Now you can." He lifted his free arm. "The stage is yours. For today, anyway."

"You—" Her throat locked up so she swallowed and tried again. "You're giving me the gift of performing."

"I am. If you want it. If it upsets you or brings back too many painful memories—"

Tara stopped his apology with a kiss, crushing the box between them. Never in her life had anyone done anything for her with so much care and thought. Her heart felt full to bursting.

Dimly, she heard cheering and remembered they had an audience. But Jace was the one blushing as she pulled back.

"Do you like it?"

"I love it." She looked around the stage, then back at him. "It's perfect."

"Then will you dance for us?"

"I'd be honored."

"Nicely done, little brother," Livia said, as Tara disappeared to the dressing room to change.

"I'm not through yet," he said, catching sight of their last guest coming through the doors of the auditorium. He hurried to greet her. "Thank you for coming."

"I admit, you've intrigued me, Mr. Applewhite."

"Come on down toward the front so you'll

have a good view." Jace escorted her himself, seeing her comfortably seated on the second row as Leo changed up the lighting scheme to something blue and wintery.

"You're a genius," Livia whispered when he took his seat.

"We'll see." He wouldn't agree with her and jinx it.

Tara stepped out onto the stage, her long blonde hair bundled neatly into a bun. The black leotard had a short, flowy, semi-translucent skirt that drifted around her long, lean legs as she moved out to take center-stage. Maybe it wasn't the perfect costume for the Sugar Plum Fairy, but none of that detracted from the picture she made as she took her position.

God, she was so beautiful.

The familiar plucked string opening of "Dance of the Sugar Plum Fairy" poured out of the sound system. On the stage, Tara began to dance, her movements as light and airy as the chimes from the celesta. And Jace forgot about his sister, forgot about his parents, forgot about everything but Tara.

She sucked him into the story, and even though the flocked trees had been decorated with another show in mind, they might as well have been a fairy wood made just for her. She barely touched the stage, her arms extended as if they held her aloft. And through it all, her face radiated joy.

The music shifted, sped up, and she launched into a series of those impossible spins, circling the stage, faster and faster, balancing on the points of her toes, until she snapped out in a regal bow as the music crescendoed to its finale.

Jace was on his feet in an instant, clapping hard enough for a dozen people. The rest of their tiny audience cheered and applauded. Austin even managed a two-fingered whistle.

Tara's smile was bright enough to light the auditorium all the way to the back row. He'd been right. It was killer. She stepped to center stage and took her graceful bow.

"Well done, Miss Honeycutt." From the row behind him, Jace's guest rose and edged out into the aisle.

Tara straightened at the unfamiliar voice, squinting against the stage lights to see who'd spoken.

Jace hurried from his seat to help her up the steps to the stage. The tap of her cane echoed in the silence.

Tara's cheeks were flushed as she waited, hands folded neatly at her waist. Her gaze flicked to his in question, but she said nothing.

"How long has it been since you danced that role?" the older woman demanded.

"I was cast for it nearly two years ago. I never had the chance to perform it until now."

"Yet you remember all the choreography."

Tara inclined her head. "I've stayed in practice as best I can."

The older woman nodded, seeming to make a decision. "Young lady, do you know who I am?"

"No ma'am, I'm afraid I don't."

"My name is Jeanette Farrar. I own Focal Pointe Dance Academy."

Tara's gaze sharpened. "A pleasure to meet you."

"It's been a very long time since I've seen a talent like yours."

Jace half expected her to take another of those fluid bows, but she only nodded politely. "Thank you."

Jeanette shifted, both hands wrapped around the head of her cane. "I understand you gave up study at SMU to come here as guardian to your siblings."

"Yes ma'am."

"And you're working as a barista at the coffee shop."

"I am."

"Ridiculous," Jeanette snapped. "You should be dancing. Such talent shouldn't be wasted."

Temper flared in Tara's eyes. "That's not—"

Jeanette rolled over her objections. "I have a dance studio. I've been unable to teach myself because of this blasted knee.

You should take my place as primary instructor."

Anger shifted to surprise. "I'm sorry?"

"You'll start after the first of the year," Jeanette said. She tapped at Jace's arm. "Help me down, young man. I've got family waiting on me and a Christmas dinner to get started."

"Wait," Tara called out. "I haven't even said yes."

The older woman turned back, one brow arched. "Are you really going to say no to doing the thing you love for a living?"

Exasperation stole a little of Tara's easy grace. "Well, no, but I'd appreciate the chance to actually give my answer instead of having it shoved down my throat."

Jeanette smiled. "You have spirit. I like that. Well then, give your answer. Do you want the job as instructor at my dance studio?"

"I do, thank you."

"Very well. As I said, you'll start after the first of the year. Long enough to give Cassie notice. Have a merry Christmas."

Tara dropped into a low curtsy. "Thank you Madam Farrar."

The gesture clearly pleased her. "Oh, I will like having a protégée again. Linda, Evan." Jeanette nodded to them both. "See you at church on Sunday."

Tara was still staring from the stage when Jace came back to her. "I think I'm in shock. Did that actually happen?"

"It did," Jace confirmed.

"So let me get this straight, you not only wangled someone to open the theater and run the lights and sound so that I could dance on *Christmas Day*, but you also managed to land me a job?"

"You landed the job. I just made the introduction."

"Has anyone ever told you you're too good to be true? Because I'm pretty sure I'm dreaming."

Jace snagged her around the waist pulling her to him. "You danced your own dream. And pulled me right on into it. Can't say I mind at all."

Tara braced her hands on his shoulders. "You realize the problem here, don't you?"

"Problem?" What hadn't he thought of?

"There's no possible way you can ever top this Christmas. Never, ever. It was beyond perfect."

Jace grinned. "Does that mean you'll be around for me to try?"

Her arms twined around his shoulder. "As long as you'll let me."

"Good. I do love a challenge. Merry Christmas, Tara."

"Merry Christmas, Jace."

CHOOSE YOUR NEXT ROMANCE!

NEXT UP IN the Wishful lineup we're moving to a second-chance romance for the slightly older crowd. Mayor Sandra Crawford had to make some tough choices back in the day—and that meant walking away from the man she really loved. But in *See You Again* he's about to walk back into her town and her life in a big, big way. Check out this silver fox romance.

If you're keen on more romance for the younger crowd—and want a front row seat to Jace and Tara's wedding, jump ahead to *Dancing Away With My Heart*. This one is a friends to lovers, second chance romance for our favorite photographer, Zach Warren. If you've got any prom or high school trauma or you love class reunion stories, this one is for you!

Also included in this volume is a special bonus! *Once Upon A Snow Day* is a Meet Cute Romance about a workaholic book editor who has to learn the value of play!

ONCE UPON A SNOW DAY

A MEET CUTE ROMANCE

There's more than snow falling this ski season.

Isabelle Lawson loves her job. Driven, dedicated, there's no room in her high-pressure life to look for love outside the pages of the books she edits. Can a fun-loving, handsome stranger change her mind?

"He wants to meet!"

Isabelle Lawson dragged her attention back to the phone. She was trying to finish typing up the edit letter that had to go out by the end of the day. "Who wants to meet?"

"Haven't you been listening? *Grant!*" Impatience and excitement snapped in Leah's voice.

Isabelle flipped through her mental roster, but the only Grants she should think of were a copy editor she knew at Random House and the hero of a romantic suspense she'd sent out a revise-and-resubmit request on three months before.

I never did hear back about that, she thought and reached for a pen to make note to follow up. "Who the heck is Grant?"

"The *doctor.*"

"Why do you need a doctor?" asked Isabelle, adding a notation to the manuscript on the screen for the author to clarify the heroine's motivation.

Leah made a frustrated noise that sounded like nothing so much as a rabid Chihuahua.

"Honestly Isabelle, can I get a moment of multi-task free attention here? I'm starting to think if it isn't about a character on a page or a deadline, you aren't aware of The World."

Given the extreme time crunch she'd been under for the last six months making certain that her new acquisitions were up to snuff and preparing for the release of not one, but two of her biggest debut authors yet, Isabelle decided that was an honest, if unflattering, observation. Guilt pinched, but publishing waited for no man, especially in the race to be the top digital press in the country.

"I'm sorry." Deliberately, she twirled in her chair until her back was to the laptop. "I swear, I'm paying attention now."

"Good. *Some* of us aren't content just reading about love. We want to actually get out there to find and experience it."

Isabelle let that gut shot sink in but didn't rise to the bait. "And Grant the doctor is…?"

"The guy I've been talking to on-line for the last three weeks."

I should have known, she thought.

Several months before, Leah had taken the plunge and signed up for on-line dating. She'd tried to drag Isabelle in with her, but Isabelle decidedly did *not* have time to waste on such things. Her career was rocketing, and she was well on her way to being exactly where she wanted to be. There'd be time enough for a man in her life somewhere down the road. Along with a hypothetical week at a spa and a two month vacation.

Chastising herself as a bad friend, she struggled to fully plug in to the conversation. "That's great!" *Isn't it?*

"He wants to go skiing."

"You kick ass at skiing, and it'll give you an opportunity to show off your curves in one of those little ski bunny outfits you like so much."

"Yes but…"

"But what? Have you gotten a creeper vibe?"

"No, not at all. He's been a total gentleman in all our chats and on the phone. But the alpaca guy was a gentleman until we met," said Leah.

Isabelle remembered the alpaca guy. He'd showed up for his first date with Leah bearing a pair of fuzzy handcuffs, a whip, and, as it turned out, the full expectation that Leah would be petting something *other* than his animals.

"If you meet him in public and take your own car, then you maintain control and your escape route should it become necessary," she said.

"I want you to come with me."

"On your *date?* Somehow I doubt Grant would be particularly enthused about that prospect."

"Not, like, *on* the date. As a covert observer so I can get your take on him. You know I value your opinion."

Paint it on thick, Isabelle thought.

"Besides," Leah continued, "if you come and you meet him, then he'll know there's a witness, and you have a face and a name to report to the police if I disappear."

"Oh, for the love of—" Isabelle rolled her eyes. "Not that I'm necessarily agreeing to this, but when is this rendezvous supposed to occur?"

"Tomorrow."

"Tomorrow! Leah, I can't just go haring off on a work day to play chaperon so you and the skiing doctor can have a snow day. I have deadlines!"

"First, there is no such thing as a non-work day for you. Second, you always have deadlines. Third, you could totally use a snow day."

"I have not had a snow day since college."

"The fact that you say that like it's a point of pride is a sad, sad thing," said Leah. "There's more to life than work, Izzy."

"Some of us actually love our jobs," she protested.

"When was the last time you looked out a window?"

"I'm looking out a window right now." Isabelle rose from her chair and pulled back the curtain so she wouldn't be a liar. "It looks white and wet and *cold.* Exactly as it has since October." Five years in Colorado and she still hadn't gotten used to the fact that winter meant actual snow for months on end. *If not for the summers,* she thought.

"Fresh air and some sun, that's what you need," Leah declared. "You can't possibly be getting enough vitamin D the way you hole up in your office, day in and day out."

"I love how this whole thing has become a favor to *me.* I am wise to your ways, my girl."

Leah huffed out a breath. "Fine. I didn't want to do this, but you leave me no choice. I'm calling in my marker from Vegas."

The breath Isabelle had taken wheezed out. "Seriously?"

"Seriously. You owe me."

"You've been sitting on that for seven years. I thought we'd agreed never to talk about it, ever again." The mere suggestion of those events had a headache brewing somewhere behind her eyes. Or maybe that was the fact that she'd been chained to her laptop since 6:30 this morning.

"I'm not talking about it. I'm just calling in the IOU."

"You really want to waste it on this?" asked Isabelle. "I mean, what if you need to murder your boss and hide the body?"

"I'll risk it," said Leah. "Tomorrow. I'll pick you up at seven. You'll come with me to the slopes, meet Grant. Once we're both assured that he's not an axe murderer, you can take my car and go home to your meetings and manuscripts. You'll probably only lose out on a couple of hours of work, tops."

Isabelle sighed. "I'll see you at seven."

War was serious business. This particular war had been waged for more than fifteen years, on battlegrounds ranging from football fields to baseball diamonds to basketball courts. Today it was racquetball and Brandon Burgan was caught in a tie, which was, to his mind, every bit as bad as losing. He wiped impatiently at the sweat dripping into his eyes as he waited for the next incoming projectile.

Thwack! The ball bounced off the wall of the court and came hurtling toward his head. With a twist and a mighty backhand, Brandon sent it winging back toward Travis with all the ferocity of a Viking berserker.

"Point!" he shouted as it sailed past his friend's racquet with inches to spare. The spurt of momentary victory was sweet and merited a little trash talk. "Getting sloppy, pal. You too busy being moony-eyed over Alicia to keep your head in the game?"

"Oh, it is *on,* pretty boy." Travis retrieved the ball and served.

Brandon returned his volley. "Whipped. That's what you are."

"No *such,*" Travis slapped the ball for emphasis, "thing. You're just jealous I'm getting regular, adult female company."

Brandon snorted at that and, for a couple of minutes, the only sounds were battle cries, the squeak of shoes, and the slap of racquet against ball. The music of friendship and competition.

Travis edged ahead by two points. "Take that," he said, with a little victory strut and point of his racquet.

"A temporary state of affairs," Brandon assured him with a cheerful flash of his middle finger. He tossed the ball to serve.

The jaunty strum of a banjo echoed off the court walls.

"Time out," called Travis, striding across to their pile of gear in the corner.

"Seriously? Haven't you heard of the *Do Not Disturb* function? It's 6:45. Who the hell is calling you this early?"

Travis didn't dignify that with a response as he reached simultaneously for a towel and his phone. "Abernathy."

That meant it was work. It was always work with Travis. Well, work or Alicia these days. She was a nice girl and a good match for Travis.

Brandon just wished Travis had a little more free time to split between them. Knowing he was likely to be a while, Brandon passed the one-sided conversation by seeing how long he could bounce the ball on his racquet without dropping it.

Couldn't pay me enough to put up with that crap, he thought. And, in fact, they hadn't. No amount of money or corner office had been enough to make him endure the suits, the endless hours, and the stress. Which was why his buddy was the lawyer and Brandon had tossed his law degree only a year after passing the bar. These days he contented himself with being a freelancer, working quite blissfully on his own doing graphic design.

He'd made it to twenty-seven bounces without dropping the ball by the time Travis hung up. "You're surgically attached to that thing, man. It's not healthy to be that connected."

"If I wasn't connected, I wouldn't have just found out that court is canceled for the day.

Judge Haygert has the stomach flu. This is awesome."

Brandon lifted a brow. "Probably not to Judge Haygert."

Travis waved him off. "Better him than me. I can get a jump start on that brief for the Wilson case."

Shaking his head, Brandon crossed the court and plucked the phone out of Travis's hand. "You're wasting a golden opportunity."

"Hey, give me that." Travis tried to nab the phone but Brandon just danced back and held it out of reach. "A golden opportunity for what?"

"To take a snow day. There's six inches of fresh powder out there. Let's hit the slopes."

The mix of guilt and desire on his friend's face was just pitiful. "I should really—"

"You should really take advantage and have some fun. You've been working your ass off to make partner since you joined the firm. C'mon."

"That would be how one actually *makes* partner," Travis pointed out.

"Dude, don't be such a suit."

"You haven't seen a suit since your mom's second wedding."

"And hallelujah for it," said Brandon with feeling. "But the point remains, people are more productive when they take actual time *off* to have *fun.*"

"Easy for you to say. You're your own boss." But Brandon could tell he was wavering.

"All the more reason for you to take advantage of this unexpected gift of a day. Who knows when you'll get another day off?"

Travis rubbed the towel over his head. "You're not giving my phone back until I agree to this, are you?"

"Nope," said Brandon equably, grabbing a water and chugging.

"How 'bout we make a wager. I win this match, you give me my phone and I go into the office and get ahead so that I can maybe actually have a Saturday off for the first time in God knows when. You win, we go skiing today."

"I am duty-bound to kick your ass to save you from yourself."

Terms agreed upon, they took their positions and resumed battle. With a two point lead, Travis was cocky. Racquetball was his sport, and he was already semi-distracted by whatever brief his mind had already started working on the moment he took that call. So he didn't expect the brutal comeback that led to Brandon trouncing him 11-8.

Bracing his hands on his thighs, Travis worked on catching his breath. "What the hell, man."

"For your…own…good," managed Brandon. He tossed a bottle of water toward Travis, who barely caught it before it crashed into his head. "Hydrate. We've got a mountain to ski."

"There he is!" Leah bounced in the driver's seat.

"Which one?"

"Black coat, gorgeous, wavy blond hair."

Isabelle scanned the people milling on the sidewalk and picked out at least three guys that fit that description. But only one of them was checking out the parking lot and rocking nervously on his heels. He got points for not looking like he thought he was God's gift, though certainly those shoulders ranked high in the eye candy department.

Leah whipped the car into a space and took a deep breath. "How do I look?"

Isabelle surveyed her from head to foot. Leah was one of those people who actually managed to look svelte rather than fat in ski clothes. "Like you're going to melt the snowcap and knock his ski boots off."

Leah grinned. "Come on."

Isabelle knew her well enough to see the nerves build as they crossed the parking lot. Not that they'd show to the Slavic-eyed hottie watching her approach.

His face brightened as she stepped up, as if he couldn't quite believe his good fortune. Leah?"

"Hi."

Grant the doctor took her hand and leaned in to buss her cheek. "It's good to finally meet you in person."

They beamed at each other.

Definitely not an axe murderer vibe, thought Isabelle with a mix of amusement and something she refused to categorize as envy. No sense in envy when there was no time to do anything about it.

When the moment stretched on without either of them looking away, Isabelle took a step closer and cleared her throat.

Leah glanced at her in apparent surprise. "Oh, sorry."

"Hi," said Isabelle into the awkward silence.

Grant seemed to clue in that she was with Leah. "And this is…?"

Isabelle offered her hand and a smile. "The witness. Isabelle Lawson."

Grant shot an amused look at Leah as he took it. "Sensible." He gestured back toward the parking lot. "Would you like to snap a picture of my license plate?"

Leah's cheeks pinked. "Sorry. I had a bad experience. One restraining order a year is my limit."

The humor vanished. "Oh geez." Grant held up his hand in a Boy Scout salute. "I swear I'm truly single, no criminal record, one of three children, born and raised within spitting distance of Yosemite. I've held a steady job since I got out of medical school and have never had a restraining order taken out against me or been charged with any crime."

"Then you're already ahead by leaps and bounds," said Isabelle.

"Will you join us on the slopes?" he asked.

Points for not sounding reluctant about that, she thought. "I think I'll pass."

"You don't ski?" asked Grant.

"I'm from Florida. We don't ski except on water. Give me eighty degrees and a wakeboard, I'm your girl. This," she waved to encompass the mountains behind them, "is not my bag."

"I keep saying I'll teach her," said Leah, "but she keeps turning me down."

"Yeah, we both know how that turned out the last time I let you try. Your version of the bunny slopes leaves me quaking in my metaphoric boots. You go enjoy your black diamond runs and leave me to the hot chocolate."

"Black diamond, huh?" asked Grant with interest. "I was all set to take it easy on you."

"Aw, that's sweet," Leah crooned, "but you can eat my powder."

"I like a confident woman," he said. "Let's get your gear."

Hiding a smile, Isabelle pulled out her phone to check her email as she fell into step behind them. There was one from the cover artist for one of the debut authors. As Grant and Leah kept up a steady banter on the way to the car, Isabelle quickly responded with tweaks to the design. The next acquisitions meeting had been pushed back a week. While they unloaded Leah's skis and poles, Isabelle updated her calendar and made additional notes about what needed to be added to the agenda. By the time they'd strapped Leah into boots, and made their way back to the path up to the lift, she and Grant had obviously all but forgotten Isabelle.

She cupped her hands around her mouth and called after them, "Have fun!"

Still deep in conversation with Grant, Leah lifted a hand in a wave but didn't turn around. Isabelle stood watching them while they snapped into their skis and made their way to the lift. By all appearances, they were well-matched, and Leah would have a good date, with a positive forecast for more in the future. After the long line of stinkers, she totally deserved it.

"And my work here is done," murmured Isabelle. Smiling and ready to get back to work, she trudged through the snowpack back to Leah's Subaru. Only when she reached into her pocket and found it empty but for her phone did she realize she'd never gotten the keys from Leah.

"Crap!" She spun back toward the lift in time to see the lime green of Leah's jacket being carried away.

It would be fine. She'd call Leah and get the keys when they made it to the bottom of their first run. She'd just grab a cup of cocoa and—

Isabelle turned back to the car, spying her purse in the floorboard of the passenger side. On the off chance that Leah had forgotten to lock it during her flirtation, Isabelle checked all the doors. No dice. And of course there was no hide-a-key in the wheel well.

"Awesome."

Finger hovering over the speed dial, she paused. Maybe she shouldn't actually call while they were on the lift. Surely wiggling around digging for a phone while a zillion feet in the air was a bad idea. Leah might drop the phone. Or worse. No, she'd send a text. Leah was good about checking.

You still have the car keys. Find me when you get to the bottom of your run.

Isabelle hit *Send.*

Now what?

Who knew how long it would take them to get back down the mountain? She *still* had those deadlines she'd mentioned yesterday.

Resigned, she trudged toward the picnic tables at the refreshment pavilion settled at the base of the slopes. From there she'd be able to watch for Leah. This early, no one had cleared them of the previous night's snow. With a broad sweep of her arm, Isabelle cleared a space to sit. Still wet and she was in jeans, not ski pants. Tugging her hat off, she laid it down and sat, hoping the knit was enough to keep her butt relatively dry. Then she popped the stylus out of her phone, pulled up the latest of her submissions, and settled in to work and wait.

"Don't answer that," warned Brandon as muffled banjos rang out from Travis' coat pocket.

Travis ignored him and checked the caller ID. "It's work. I have to answer it."

"Even *more* reason not to answer."

"Abernathy."

Brandon rolled his eyes and headed for the refreshment pavilion. If he was going to have to wait while Travis talked whoever through whatever, he was going to do it with coffee. Standing at the back of the line, he scanned the slopes. It was a beautiful day, perfect weather, fresh powder. And, being a weekday, the mountain wouldn't be over-crowded.

Travis had stopped halfway from the parking lot. He was pacing a short loop, his free hand scooping irritably through his hair. The expression on his face didn't bode well.

I should never have let him have the phone back, Brandon thought. Clearly there was no saving him from the job without completely disconnecting him from civilization and technology.

Travis wasn't the only one, he noted. A

dozen feet away, a woman at one of the picnic tables was also hunched over her phone, stylus tapping at the screen. Glossy, dark brown hair spilled out from the fur-lined hood pulled up over her head. As he watched, she looked up toward the slopes and the parking lot. He had a brief, tantalizing view of delicate features and long-lidded eyes before she looked down again and went back to whatever she was doing.

With those jeans and hiking boots, she clearly wasn't dressed for skiing, so what was she doing here? *Waiting for someone?* Brandon wondered. Not enjoying the views, that was for sure. And that was a damned shame. At least he'd saved himself from that kind of technological suck. If he had his way, he'd eventually manage to do the same for Travis.

At the crunch of snow, he turned to see the man in question, an apologetic expression on his face. Today was clearly not going to be the day he got saved.

"No," said Brandon, pointing at him. "No,

you are *not* about to back out on me now. We're already here."

"I'm sorry, man," said Travis. "But that was one of the senior partners. He wants to pull me in as co-council on a huge corporate case. I have to go in."

"You are full of suck," declared Brandon. "Abandoning me in my hour of need."

"Hour of need my ass."

"Okay, fine, *your* hour of need. The system's gonna kill you."

Travis began backing away, lifting his hands in a gesture of acknowledgment. "We'll reschedule. I'll plan a day off in a few weeks, and we'll come back."

How many times had he heard that since Travis had joined Rigel, Williams, and Stone?

"You don't *plan* for perfect powder," Brandon insisted. "You embrace it when it happens."

"Sorry, Bran!"

On a whim, Brandon bent and scooped up a palmful of snow.

"Hey now," said Travis. "There's no call for that."

He felt a slow smile spread over his face as he packed his ammo. "There's every call for this. I won this snow day and now you're bailing. You gotta pay the penalty."

He let the snowball fly with all the momentum of an outfielder aiming to cut off a base runner, feeling the sing of muscle as it left his hand. Travis darted to the side, just out of the line of fire, and Brandon watched with horror as the snowball hurtled by him and slammed against the head of the brunette at the picnic table.

She squeaked in surprise and dropped the phone.

"Oh, shit," he muttered.

Slowly, oh so slowly, her shoulders dropped from the defensive hunch and she turned her head—hoodless now—to look at Travis. His eyes were round as saucers and he was already pointing back toward Brandon. She shifted her attention, and Brandon found himself snared by a pair of gorgeous brown eyes, slitted with temper.

Wow. For a moment, that was all he could think. *Now there's a face a man could get lost in.* Then his brain re-engaged and he was striding across to her, spewing apology. "I am so sorry. I wasn't aiming at you. I was aiming for him, and the coward moved, and I—"

"Stop right there," she said, lifting a hand like a traffic cop.

Brandon did.

The woman brushed the snow from the long fall of her hair. She flicked a glance at Travis, who'd retrieved her phone and now held it out like a peace offering. Ignoring him, she bent. At first, Brandon thought she was picking up the stylus, but instead she began to gather together snow. His lips twitched, but he held his ground. He'd totally earned whatever payback she was about to dish out.

She dug deep, clearing away the light, fresh powder for the wetter snow beneath. When she had a mass approximately the size of a small cantaloupe, she took two steps forward and hurled it. From a mere six feet away, the ball splattered against the fleece beneath Brandon's open parka. Cold, wet shrapnel struck him in the face but did nothing to erase the smile. He had to appreciate a woman with a finely-tuned sense of revenge.

Retaliation delivered, his inadvertent victim briskly knocked snow off her mittens and turned back to Travis to collect her phone. "Thank you," she said politely.

Travis, face as sober as a judge, sketched a slight bow. "I do apologize. Under normal circumstances, I'd never choose self-preservation over a lady, but I just didn't see you."

"Accidents happen," she said equably. "You weren't the one pretending you were ten." She slanted a glance back at Brandon.

"Quite right. I'm the grown up, who is—" he checked his watch, "going to be very late for work."

"You and me both," she said.

Travis paused, his desire to reassert his

chivalry apparently over-riding his internal clock. "Oh, can I give you a ride or something?"

"No, you go," said Brandon stepping up to make his own effort at chivalry. "You're already late. If the lady needs a lift, I'll do it. I'm the one not on a time clock." He offered the woman a smile. "It's the least I can do."

"I can vouch that he's not a lunatic," Travis told her. "And he's had all his shots."

"I'm even housebroken," Brandon added.

The corner of her mouth quirked at that, but she shook her head. "I'll provide my own lift, thanks, just as soon as my friend gets back with the keys."

With a silent wave, Travis trudged toward the parking lot. Brandon's attention was solidly on Miss Brown Eyes. "Then at least let me buy you a cup of coffee or cocoa while you wait."

"Now that I'll take you up on."

He made an *after you* gesture toward the refreshment pavilion. As she walked, her attention immediately zeroed in on the phone.

"It's not damaged, is it?" he asked, falling

into step beside her.

"No. Battery's nearly zapped, though." A thread of anxiety laced her voice.

Tech addict on the verge of losing her fix? he wondered. "They don't last as well in the cold."

"Neither do I." A shiver underscored the statement. He realized she looked half-frozen, a state of affairs certainly not improved by snowball assault.

"Well, I can do something about that, at least." Brandon shrugged out of his parka and draped it around her shoulders.

She jolted. "I can't take your coat."

"One of us dressed for this weather," he said, stepping up to the window. "Coffee or cocoa?"

"Cocoa," she said, her face still fixed in a puzzled frown.

Brandon just smiled and ordered. After a moment, she shifted to slip her arms through the sleeves and zipped it closed. The lower half of her face disappeared behind the collar. As soon as she lowered her arms, her hands disappeared inside the sleeves. Damn, that was cute.

"Thank you."

"I gather you didn't expect to be out here today," he said, carrying the drinks back to one of the picnic tables.

"Not for long." She tugged off her mittens and wrapped slim fingers around the cup. "I came with a friend to meet her date and verify he wasn't an axe murderer. But I forgot to get the keys before they hit the lift, so I'm waiting for her to get back to the bottom."

"How long have you been waiting?"

"Going on two hours now." She took a sip of her cocoa and hissed a little.

He lifted a brow as he tested his own drink and felt his taste buds die a fiery death. "I think you may have to consider the possibility that your friend didn't get the message."

Resigned, she sighed. "I'm afraid you may be right. She probably turned her phone off and didn't get my texts."

"Not much of a signal up top either. Either way, that leaves you late for work. I seriously don't mind driving you in. There's no sense in your boss being ticked at you for something that isn't your fault."

"The only boss that'll be irritated is me. I don't have a traditional eight to five job, so nobody's waiting at an office for me to show up."

"Really? Me either. I'm a graphic designer. What do you do?"

"I'm a book editor," she said.

"Here? I thought all that took place in New York."

"The lion's share does," she explained, "and I did my time in the trenches there. But with the rise of digital publishing houses, that's less a necessity. My company's parent office is actually in Denver, but I spend most of my time telecommuting from here. All of the fun, none of the traffic."

With another scan of the slopes behind them, Isabelle tugged out her phone and checked the display. She gave a low curse.

"Dead?" he asked.

"As a doornail."

"Look, my offer to drive you to wherever still stands."

"You really don't have to do that. I already exacted payback—which you were a really good sport about, by the way. The hot chocolate and loan of coat already put me in your debt."

Brandon smirked, liking the sound of that.

"You look entirely too pleased by that idea," she said, expression wary.

"Let's just say I consider it a stroke of good fortune."

"Oh yeah? How's that?"

"You're a helluva lot prettier than Travis."

Her cheeks pinked from more than the cold, which completely undermined the stern look she shot him. "I get the feeling you're a helluva lot more incorrigible."

"Guilty," he said, unrepentant. "Look, if you're gonna be stuck here incommunicado and unable to keep working, you might as well have some fun. Take a snow day. With me."

"You sound like Leah."

"Leah sounds like a sensible woman. How

about it? You said you owe me."

"I don't ski," she said.

"There's more to do in snow than ski," said Brandon.

"You don't even know me."

"I'm Brandon. And you're...?"

"Isabelle."

"There. You're Isabelle, the workaholic book editor. Now we've been properly introduced."

Her exasperated sigh was punctuated by a half laugh. "You're persistent, aren't you?"

"Competition junkie and ex-lawyer," he confirmed.

"Why would you want to spend the day with me?" She seemed well and truly baffled by the idea.

"Well, apart from the fact that you're interesting, intelligent, and quite willing to dish out as good as you get—which I appreciate, by the way—you remind me of how I used to be, and I consider it a personal mission in life to save workaholics from themselves. Travis is a lost cause today, but you're not. So, how 'bout it?"

"Where are we going?" asked Isabelle.

"Equipment rental to check out our options," he said, zipping up the jacket she'd given back. "Under ordinary circumstances, I'd take you ice skating, but there's nowhere to do that at this particular resort."

"Too bad. That I can sort of do without breaking anything vital."

"Doubly too bad," said Brandon, flashing a flirtatious grin. "I'd enjoy teaching you."

"Do a lot of that, do you?"

"Not especially, but it's a classic winter move for a reason."

Isabelle made a non-committal hum but found herself rather unwillingly charmed. She couldn't figure out how he'd done that, how he'd convinced her to spend this time with him. Hot, flirtatious guys were Leah's department, not hers. Yet here she was.

"So," he asked, "is there anybody special

who's going to be upset by my monopolizing your time today?"

That was as good an opening as she'd ever get to test him. Better to find out now that he was typical before this went any further. "Well, there's Devin."

"Devin?"

Isabelle felt her lips quirk. "Mmm. He's a firefighter. Has some issues, but he's working through them. Heart of gold."

Brandon actually stopped.

Isabelle tried to hold back the grin as she pivoted to face him. "Of course, he's in love with Tess, which, if pattern holds, means he ought to be admitting it to himself in another ten or twelve thousand words. But probably not until her life is threatened by the serial arsonist on the loose."

"I—" He didn't seem to know how to reply to that, and the look on his face had her laughing.

"Devin is my current book boyfriend."

"Book boyfriend?" Brandon repeated.

"Devin's the hero of the sub I was reading before you clocked me. Pretty sure I'll be making an offer on it if his author nails the ending. But that depends on how she handles the arsonist." Isabelle smiled sweetly. "One of the perks of being a romance editor. I get to change boyfriends as fast as I can read and don't have to worry about them leaving dirty socks in the floor."

She waited for the sneer and smart ass remark that denigrated the genre and implied that no breathing man could live up to the fictional hype and expectations.

Brandon seemed to consider her words. "So what I'm hearing is there's nobody who will fly into a jealous rage and try to kick my ass?"

"Not presently, no."

He nodded and fell into step beside her again. "Good."

Huh. So not the reaction she was accustomed to getting from guys about her job. *Wonders will never cease.*

"So romance, huh?" The question was casual.

Isabelle didn't buy that for a minute. Next it would be *Why don't you read real books?* "Yep." *I knew he was too good to be true.*

"You do any work with Nora Roberts or Jill Shalvis?"

It was Isabelle's turn to stop. "You actually can *name* some romance authors?"

"I have a mom and sister who are rabid readers," he said. "Books didn't have genres in our house. They were just books. I read several myself when I was laid up with a broken leg several years back. Got hooked on those Eve and Roarke books. She's a real ball buster. I dig that in a woman."

Isabelle could only stare as Brandon moved up several notches in her estimation. A gentleman who actually *admitted* to reading romance? "I think I officially love your mom and sister."

"Me too. They're pretty great. So, do you?" he prompted

"Do I what?" she asked, glancing toward the sky in search of flying pigs. Somewhere in there, she'd lost the thread of the conversation.

"Work with them? 'Cause I'd win best son and brother award if I could score autographs."

"No. I don't. But I've met them at conference. I confess to having total fangirl moments when I got their autographs myself."

"Cool," he said, stepping up to the equipment hut and scanning the list of available gear. "How do you feel about tubing?"

"I don't see any ski boats around."

"I gather you're from warmer climes."

"Florida originally."

"You're a long way from home," he observed. "Up here we use them for sledding. See, they've even got these nifty two-person numbers. We'll get one of those."

"I don't know…"

"It'll be fun," he promised, shooting her another of those wide, infectious grins that invited her to share in some kind of secret joke. It scrambled her brain a little, and the next thing she knew, they were on their way up the mountain maintaining a steady stream of intelligent conversation about books as the tow cable pulled them up and up and up.

As they reached the top, she broke off the heated debate about whether Peter Jackson had done *The Hobbit* justice with his interpretation for the movies. A gorgeous vista stretched out before them, all blue against white, sparkling in the mid-morning sun. Unlike the ski slopes, no one else was around to interrupt the sensation that they were the only two people on earth. For maybe the first time in ages, all thoughts of work bled out of her mind and she simply stared.

"Wow," she breathed.

"Quite the view, isn't it?" asked Brandon, stepping up beside her. He sucked in a lungful of brisk mountain air and let it out with a sound of utter contentment.

"It is that," Isabelle murmured, looking up at him from the corner of her eye. *What the hell am I doing here?*

Brandon dragged the snow tube into position at the top of the slope and held it steady. "You want front or back?"

Isabelle hesitated. It was a long way to the bottom. She wasn't sure how she felt about the idea of hurtling down the slope at high speeds. She'd thought the trail would be all straight and pretty and groomed. The ground under that snow wasn't exactly forgiving if they crashed. At least with water you sank in. And there were trees off to the side. What if they ran into one? It wasn't like you could steer an inner tube. She supposed you'd see it coming and could roll off. But was that safe? How fast could an inner tube *go* anyway?

"There's no way back but down," he pointed out.

"Not true. If you lose your skis and drag off to the side and look pathetic, the ski patrol will eventually come and get you." Which was what had happened the one time Leah had gotten her anywhere but the bunny slopes. "There's a reason I don't ski."

Brandon didn't laugh. "Fair enough. But as we have established, this isn't skiing. It's perfectly safe. You held on just fine on the way up."

"We were going slow on the way up," she grumbled. And he'd distracted her with good conversation.

Brandon crouched to point out the handles again, then looked back at her and held out a hand. "Trust me, Isabelle."

Isabelle thought foolishly of Aladdin and his magic carpet. He had that kind of open, friendly face, which was probably how he'd talked her into this in the first place. *At least this is on the ground.*

She placed her hand in his, feeling his gloved fingers curve firmly around hers. The connection simultaneously steadied her and made her nerves jump. He had big hands. They were careful as he helped settle her behind him on the snow tube, and she was almost sorry when he let go.

"Ready?" asked Brandon.

"As I'll ever be."

"Hold on!"

Isabelle thought fleetingly of holding on to *him*. He was big and solid and so damned appealing. And she barely knew him. Quickly, she curled her hands around the rear set of handles as he shoved off.

The wind fluttered her hair as they started their descent. This wasn't so bad. Nice and easy. Pleasant, even.

Then they hit a steeper grade and began to pick up speed. Isabelle's hair whipped back and her eyes began to sting. She didn't feel entirely stable on the back end of the tube as they skittered over some bumps in the snow. Her hands fisted tighter around the handles even as Brandon whooped.

"Brace yourself! Got a little drop coming."

They caught air. Isabelle didn't know how, couldn't see past Brandon's bigger body, but she felt it in the sudden loss of friction beneath them. Then they landed with a jarring thud, and she was throwing her arms around his waist and hanging on for dear life. That shifted the balance, and the back end of the inner tube swung around so they were racing sideways down the slope.

Brandon's arms clamped down tight over hers as they began to spin. Faster and faster. Isabelle saw a blur of trees and pressed her face against his back. He was shaking. No, he was... laughing. Great whoops of laugher.

"You're crazy!" she shouted.

"Live a little!" he called back, but his laughter was interrupted by another huge jolt.

Isabelle felt her arms break free of his grip and she went flying.

They landed in a snowbank, a tangle of limbs. Brandon's face was pressed half in the snow, half against her hair. It smelled like vanilla. Aware he was crushing her, he scrambled, trying to get enough purchase to get off her. He succeeded only in straddling her body, knees on either side of her hips. She was shaking.

God, she'd been so anxious about the whole thing, and here they'd crashed. She was probably freaked out. Pushing up with both hands, he asked, "Are you okay? Are you hurt?"

Isabelle sucked in a good breath…and began to laugh.

Brandon stopped moving, too caught up in the delighted curve of her mouth and the humor sparking in those gorgeous brown eyes. The smile transformed her serious face into something that hit him low in the gut. *I am in serious trouble,* he thought.

Breath still hitching with helpless giggles, Isabelle said, "You look like the abominable snowman." She reached up and proceeded to brush a substantial pile of snow from his head and the right side of his face.

It didn't matter that she wore mittens. It might as well have been warm fingers against his cheek for all Brandon ceased to feel the the cold.

That mouth. God, he wanted to taste her. He dragged his gaze from her lips back to her eyes.

Awareness swam into them, her pupils springing wide. She stopped laughing. Her hand slid from his cheek to his shoulder but didn't push him away. Brandon held very still, enjoying the sense of expectation as the moment spun out, his heart starting to gallop. Eyes open and focused on hers, he started to lower. Isabelle gave a quick, involuntary hitch of breath, parting her lips.

Using the tension in his braced muscles, Brandon shoved up, managing to get one foot under him enough to rise. Better to keep her guessing, keep her off balance. He had a fleeting moment to see confusion flash across her face before he let himself topple like a tree into the snow behind him. Isabelle's unsteady breath had him fighting a smile. Mission accomplished.

To give her a moment to settle and cool his own unexpected arousal, he moved his limbs in a wide arc.

"What on earth are you doing?" she asked.

"Making a snow angel." When she said nothing, he lifted his head to find her half sitting up in the snow bank looking puzzled. "Haven't you ever made a snow angel before?"

"We didn't exactly have an abundance of white stuff in the panhandle."

"That's just tragic," said Brandon sitting up. "Come on. You're already covered in snow. Might as well correct that serious oversight in your childhood education."

She shot him another of those mildly exasperated smiles. "You're a funny guy, Brandon."

"I do try. C'mon."

Despite her Very Serious Grownup attitude, she flopped down a few feet away in the snow and proceeded to make her snow angel. He liked that about her. He found he liked a great many things about her and said a brief, silent prayer of thanks that Travis had bailed.

"Let's get you up before your jeans soak through," he said. Pulling her up was easy. Tucking her against his side to study her efforts was easier, and the arm she slipped around his

waist was progress, payment for denying himself that kiss.

"A perfect first attempt," he pronounced.

"Even a workaholic can learn new tricks."

"You're a good student."

"Leah would argue with you on that. She
says I work too hard, too much."

Brandon released her and went to retrieve
the snow tube. "I say that about Travis all the
time."

"But does he truly love what he does? Like
truly, passionately love it?" Isabelle asked.

He considered the question. "I don't know. I
know I didn't."

"I do. I mean, seriously, I have the best job in
the world. I get to read all the time. I get first look
at all kinds of fabulous books and get to work with
some of the most creative minds in the field. If I
work all the time, it's because I enjoy it." Brandon
could see the truth of it glinting in her eyes, in the
animated gestures of her hands as she spoke.

"That is a great and powerful gift, something that most people never get. Most folks end up working something just for a paycheck, not because it's their passion."

"Is that why you're an ex?" she asked.

"What?"

"Earlier, you said you were an ex-lawyer."

"Oh, well, that's a story."

"I've got time," said Isabelle. She looked at the flat expanse of snow in front of them. "I don't have a lot of experience at this, but I'm guessing we'll have to walk a bit before we get to enough incline to get going again."

Brandon tipped his head in acknowledgment and began to pick his way back toward the slope. "I figured I'd be a great lawyer," he began. Because she was close and he wanted to keep her there, he grabbed her hand with his free one and swung it companionably between them. "I've got a competitive streak a mile wide —Travis will tell you. We've been one-upping each other since high school. And as you already know, I'm naturally persuasive."

"Oh, obviously," she said, smirking.

"Travis and I went through together, and I did great in school. School's just another competition to get to the top. And I always wanted to be at the top. Then I got out."

"Rude awakening?" She said it with the kind of rueful smile that suggested she'd had one of her own.

"You could say that."

"Did you find out you were actually a little fish in a really big ocean?"

"No, though I guess there was some of that. I was…disillusioned. The law isn't about truth or justice, and it's not even about what's right. Turns out I care a lot more about those things than winning. It's a broken system, and certainly it's better than nothing, but it isn't what I wanted—what I *needed* it to be, and I didn't like who it made me. So I got out. Travis went on to pursue partnership in a prestigious firm, and I struck out on my own in a totally new field."

"Do you like graphic design?"

"I do," he said. "I kind of fell into it. I've always been something of a tech geek. I love playing with new software. When I found myself at loose ends, a friend asked me to design some stuff for her new business. She loved the concepts I had and recommended me to someone else, and it kind of went down the chain until it just made sense to formalize it. I like the freedom and creativity of it, and the fact that apart from making the client happy, there's no right or wrong, no value judgment."

"Do you miss the competition?"

"Oh there's still competition. Awards to be won, accounts to bid on… And there are plenty of other pluses."

"Such as?"

"There's no dress code and the schedule is pretty awesome."

"Sounds like a win on all counts."

"That awesome schedule meant I was here to hang out with you, so I'd say yes, definite win."

"Even though you wanted to hang out with Travis?"

"I think Fate is a helluva lot smarter than I

am," he said.

Isabelle laughed. "You are a charmer."

"I try," he said, with faux modesty. They reached the incline again. "So, are you willing to brave the slopes again or are you done with snow tubing for the day?"

"I'm game to try again. But this time, *I'm* riding in front."

"Sure you don't want another run?" asked Brandon.

"Not without ski pants," said Isabelle. "I stopped feeling my butt two runs back."

He tipped his head to check out her behind. "Still there, still pretty damned perfect. But hot beverage station it is. And some food. I could eat a moose. Let me just turn this thing in."

She waited while he walked to the equipment hut to return the snow tube. It had been an unexpectedly fabulous morning with a wholly unexpected guy. She kept thinking she had him pegged, then he'd say or do something to turn her assumptions on their ears.

Well, they do have that saying about assuming, she mused.

Being wrong had never been so appealing. Except for that almost kiss. She'd been certain he was going to do it, and she'd welcomed it. There was no question he was interested. But he'd pulled back. God, how she wished he hadn't. But perhaps another opportunity would present itself before the day was through.

Brandon started to turn from the equipment window. A snowball smacked him in the back. "Hey!" He whirled around, a mock stern expression fixed on her.

Isabelle opened her hands to show innocence and looked in the direction the missile had come from. A quartet of kids, maybe nine or ten years old were running, shrieking, and lobbing more snowballs at each other. One of them, a boy in a bright yellow jacket and a black beanie was doing his best to pretend he wasn't involved.

She crossed to Brandon, keeping an eye on Yellow Jacket. "I think we can take them."

He send her a sideways glance. "Is your aim decent beyond six feet?"

"Ten years of summer league softball. What I lack in speed and force, I make up for with accuracy."

"In that case, I like the way you think." He bent and scooped up snow. "Hey kid!"

Yellow Jacket turned just in time for the snowball to splat against his shoulder. His stunned surprise gave way to a grin as he rallied his friends to the cause. Within moments Isabelle and Brandon were engaged in an all out war. They took cover behind a trash can, gathering ammo and launching it toward the enemy. Outnumbered, they took as many shots as they made, but they were laughing, cat calling as they did it.

When the barrage stopped, Isabelle hunkered down behind their makeshift bunker for a powwow. "Do you think it's safe?"

Brandon dared a peek. "They're gathered

behind that drift over there. Pretty sure they're stockpiling ammo."

"What's the plan?"

"This thing isn't great cover. If we can sneak around to that other snowdrift, we could circle around behind them. They'd be sitting ducks."

"There's no cover for covert approach. You'll have to run for it."

"True enough."

"You go first," she said.

"Fine, fine. My plan. I'm the man and all that." He darted in, brushed a lightning fast kiss across her cheek. "For luck." Then he made a break for it.

The fresh volley of snowballs started immediately, pelting him from head to toe until he stumbled—entirely on purpose, she was certain —into the snowbank and adopted a posture of defeat. Unwilling to abandon her comrade in arms, Isabelle followed, enduring the bombardment against back, shoulders, and legs until she too collapsed into the snowbank. At least, that had been her intention.

Brandon snagged her on the way down so she fell on top of him instead. "Imagine meeting you here," he said, hooking his arms around her waist.

"Hi," she said softly. She imagined she felt the heat of his body through all their layers of clothes.

His gray eyes twinkled with amusement. Isabelle's gaze zeroed in on his mouth, curved in amusement. Looked like that second opportunity was going to present itself after all.

Hallelujah.

"Isabelle!"

The voice filtered through, a dim, distant irritation. At first she thought she imagined it, but the call came again, distracting her from the lure of Brandon's mouth. She lifted her head and caught sight of Leah.

Of course, she shows up now.

Swearing silently, Isabelle scrambled up. Away from Brandon's warmth, she shivered almost immediately. Or maybe that was the intense, focused expression on his face as he took her hand and let her tug him to his feet. As soon as he was vertical, she started to pull away, but he tightened his grip on her hand.

A snowball hit him in the back and he shot a smile at the kids. "Cease fire, guys!"

Leah and Grant carved their way to a quick stop beside them in a tandem move that looked choreographed. "I just got your texts! I'm so sorry!"

I'm not, thought Isabelle.

"No, it's fine, I..." Isabelle looked up at Brandon, feeling a faint frisson of panic when he refused to release her hand. "Um, this is Brandon. Brandon, Leah. And her date Grant."

Brandon nodded hello as Leah's gaze swept him from head to toe, lingering on their joined hands. Her mouth quirked in amused speculation.

"And how did this," Leah waved a hand to encompass their joined hands, "happen?"

"There was an incident with a snowball," she explained.

Leah waited for further elaboration, but Isabelle offered none. She knew perfectly well she'd be grilled later and preferred that to happen in private.

"Well," she said, "looks like you ended up taking something of a snow day after all."

"It seemed a better alternative to freezing my butt off while waiting for you," said Isabelle.

"She'll do a lot if she's bribed with hot beverages," said Brandon.

Leah lifted a perfectly manicured brow.

"Snow tubing," Isabelle hurried to say, blood rushing into her cheeks.

Her friend beamed at Brandon in approval. "Excellent. Maybe I should strand you at a ski resort more often."

And just like that, all the deadlines and manuscripts and piles of work she'd blown off came crashing back into her mind. "Just so that you don't continue to do so today…the keys?" asked Isabelle.

"Right." Leah tugged off a glove, dug them out of her coat, and handed them over.

Isabelle looked from Leah to Grant and

back again. "So you two are good?"

They exchanged delighted smiles. "We're great," said Leah. "Grant will drop me home later."

Given the waves of chemistry pulsing off them, Isabelle suspected it would be much, much later. *Good for you, girl.*

"Okay, well, have fun. Thanks for bringing back the keys."

"Sorry about the mix-up." Leah shot a look at Brandon. "Or maybe not. See you later." With a wave, she and Grant shoved off and headed back toward the lift.

Isabelle stared after them a lot longer than necessary to avoid looking at Brandon. The snowball fight had fallen apart, the kids wandering off to other pursuits. Whatever ease they'd found with each other over the last few hours had vanished. She half wished he'd tackle her into the snow bank or lob another snowball to startle her out of workaholic mode again, but he made no move to do either as she turned to him.

"I should go," she said. *Talk me out of it.*

"Current book boyfriend won't be put off any longer, huh?"

A smile fluttered at the edge of her lips. "He's been awfully patient today."

Brandon nodded, conceding defeat. "I'll walk you to your car."

Damn it.

On the walk back to the parking lot, Isabelle reflected that Leah had truly craptastic timing. Her appearance had broken whatever spell Brandon had woven over the day, reminding her of all the things she'd neglected for this un-planned romp in the snow. She wished Leah's phone had died, as hers had. Glancing up at Brandon out of the corner of her eye, she wished a lot of things. That he hadn't pulled back up on the mountain. That she hadn't been interrupted. Now both moments were past, and she didn't know how to recapture the relaxed, casual flirtation.

They reached the Subaru.

"Well, here we are," she said.

"Here we are," said Brandon.

Isabelle fiddled with the keys in her mitten-less hand, wondering if she could work up the guts to try to kiss him and if she could pull it off without the whole thing being weird and awkward.

"I had a lot of fun today. I'm not that great at fun, so…thanks." She dared a look up at him.

His expression was sober, but she could tell he was laughing with his eyes. It got her back up and killed some of the nerves.

"What?" she demanded.

"That's a sad, sad state, not being any good at fun," he said.

Embarrassment and irritation warred, and Isabelle dropped her gaze.

"I'm duty bound, as an ambassador of fun, to see that you continue with your lessons."

Her head shot up at that.

"So, I'm gonna need your last name and phone number," he finished. His mouth quirked. "For professional purposes only."

Isabelle felt her lips twitch. "Naturally. It's

Lawson."

He pulled out his phone and waited as she gave her number.

"Mine's dead," she said, "so you'll have to call me."

Brandon punched something in. "There. Now you'll have a text from me when yours has juice again." He shoved the phone into his pocket.

"Good thinking." She knew she'd be plugging the thing into a charger as soon as she got into the car.

"You have work, so I'll see you around."

"See you around," she said.

He stepped back and started toward the slopes again.

A sense of disappointment zinged through her. Before she could think better of it, she called after him, "Hey Brandon?"

"Yeah?"

She checked her watch, did some mental calculations. "Devin and Tess should be firmly ensconced in their happily ever after by six-thirty. I've gotta eat. Do you have plans for dinner?"

He smiled and crossed back to her. "Just to meet you. One condition, though."

"What's that?"

"We start with dessert first." Brandon stepped close, boxing her in against the car so she had to lift her head to keep his gaze.

"I'm amenable to that," she said.

"Great," he murmured. One corner of his mouth kicked up as he slid a hand beneath the fall of her hair to cup her nape and tip her face up to his. His other hand curved around her hip.

Isabelle expected sweet, maybe a bit of playful, as that was the impression he'd given all day. But Brandon surprised her yet again. He took his time closing the small distance between them, his gaze caressing her face before fixing on hers. Her pulse jumped in anticipation and nerves quivered in her belly. Waiting. Waiting.

He kept his eyes open, something she'd read

about but always thought strange. Somehow it intensified the sensation of warmth as his lips slanted over hers. The sensation spread down her body until she forgot the wind and snow and cold. It was like being wrapped in melted caramel, delicious and decadent. On a little purr, she rose to her toes, running her hands up his chest and shoulders to thread into the hair that escaped his hat. Brandon tugged her closer, settling his mouth more firmly over hers, kissing her as if he had all the time in the world to make sure he did the job justice.

Isabelle didn't know who pulled back. She was pretty sure the world was spinning drunkenly around them and was positive her feet weren't actually on the ground.

Brandon dropped his temple to hers. "Wow."

She let out another hum of approval. "Who would've thought the payback for Vegas would be so sweet."

"Huh?"

Isabelle shook her head to clear it. "Long story, that. I'll tell you about it over dinner."

OTHER BOOKS BY KAIT NOLAN

A complete and up-to-date list of all my books can be found at https://kaitnolan.com.

THE MISFIT INN SERIES
SMALL TOWN FAMILY ROMANCE

- *When You Got A Good Thing* (Kennedy and Xander)
- *Til There Was You* (Misty and Denver)

- *Those Sweet Words* (Pru and Flynn)
- *Stay A Little Longer* (Athena and Logan)
- *Bring It On Home* (Maggie and Porter)

RESCUE MY HEART SERIES
SMALL TOWN MILITARY ROMANCE

- *Baby It's Cold Outside* (Ivy and Harrison)
- *What I Like About You* (Laurel and Sebastian)
- *Bad Case of Loving You* (Paisley and Ty prequel)
- *Made For Loving You* (Paisley and Ty)

MEN OF THE MISFIT INN
SMALL TOWN SOUTHERN ROMANCE

- *Let It Be Me* (Emerson and Caleb)
- *Our Kind of Love* (Abbey and Kyle)

WISHFUL SERIES

SMALL TOWN SOUTHERN ROMANCE

- *Once Upon A Coffee* (Avery and Dillon)
- *To Get Me To You* (Cam and Norah)
- *Know Me Well* (Liam and Riley)
- *Be Careful, It's My Heart* (Brody and Tyler)
- *Just For This Moment* (Myles and Piper)
- *Wish I Might* (Reed and Cecily)
- *Turn My World Around* (Tucker and Corinne)
- *Dance Me A Dream* (Jace and Tara)
- *See You Again* (Trey and Sandy)
- *The Christmas Fountain* (Chad and Mary Alice)
- *You Were Meant For Me* (Mitch and Tess)
- *A Lot Like Christmas* (Ryan and Hannah)
- *Dancing Away With My Heart* (Zach and Lexi)

WISHING FOR A HERO SERIES (A WISHFUL SPINOFF SERIES)
SMALL TOWN ROMANTIC SUSPENSE

- *Make You Feel My Love* (Judd and Autumn)
- *Watch Over Me* (Nash and Rowan)
- *Can't Take My Eyes Off You* (Ethan and Miranda)
- *Burn For You* (Sean and Delaney)

MEET CUTE ROMANCE
SMALL TOWN SHORT ROMANCE

- *Once Upon A Snow Day*
- *Once Upon A New Year's Eve*
- *Once Upon An Heirloom*
- *Once Upon A Coffee*
- *Once Upon A Campfire*
- *Once Upon A Rescue*

SUMMER CAMP
CONTEMPORARY ROMANCE

- *Once Upon A Campfire*
- *Second Chance Summer*

ABOUT KAIT

Kait is a Mississippi native, who often swears like a sailor, calls everyone sugar, honey, or darlin', and can wield a bless your heart like a saber or a Snuggie, depending on requirements.

You can find more information on this

RITA ® Award-winning author and her books on her website http://kaitnolan.com. While you're there, sign up for her newsletter so you don't miss out on news about new releases!

www.ingramcontent.com/pod-product-compliance
Lightning Source LLC
Chambersburg PA
CBHW070530100726
47907CB00004B/1062